THREE
MINUTES MORE

EDWARD R. O'DELL

Table of Contents

Chapter 1: What is Heaven?

When I was younger, I occasionally marveled at the promise of Heaven. Living in the "Bible Belt," that promise has been impressed upon me ever since I can remember. And while I do believe in it, I never, before tonight, had reason to seriously consider that I might be going to meet God. But this evening's events have left me hurt pretty badly, and while I am hoping it's not my time to go, I have always heard it can't hurt to be prepared.

That said, if this is the night God does decide to take me home, I hope Heaven has a creek with lots of big crawdads in it. I figure He must like crawdads, because He sure made a lot of them!

Oddly, though I went to church enough to be known by name, I hardly ever heard Heaven actually described. Preachers and Sunday school teachers alike seemed to prefer to talk about what would happen if one didn't make it to Heaven. "You will burn for eternity. You'll pray to die, but you can't. You'll beg God to give you another chance, but He will have forever closed His ears," they said.

Granny, on the other hand, preferred to focus more on the imagery. Although I haven't seen either her or Grandpa Joe for more than a year, I doubt she

2

has lost her fervor for all things Heaven. She described it as a paradise. A beautiful, tranquil place where nothing bad can happen. "Granny talked a lot about God. In fact, she rarely uttered a sentence that didn't refer to God in some form. Even the most mundane of things, such as the arrival of one of her grandchildren to hoe her garden, prompted a "praise God!" or a "thank you, Jesus!"

Grandpa Joe used to get annoyed by what he called "her johnny-come-lately bible thumping."

According to Granny, anything that happened, good or bad, was "God's work." Grandpa Joe disagreed with her, telling her "not everything is God's work. Some of it is the work of the devil, but the vast majority of it is man's doing."

Anytime Granny challenged him on his beliefs, Grandpa Joe quickly pointed out that it wasn't until her atheist brother lay dying, begging God to forgive him, did she become a Believer. He often reminded her she lived a life of unmentionable sin for some sixty years. He told her he found it absurd she felt entitled to preach to him.

Even when not loudly discussing matters of faith, Granny found other things to yell at him about, most of which regarded either all the work he didn't get finished at the greenhouse they owned, or for not standing up for his daughter, even if he knew she was in the wrong.

Come to think of it, I can recall few civil conversations between the two. You know, I think she actually *enjoyed* yelling. I have often wondered how she could yell so much and not lose her voice. I know on those occasions in which I yelled too much, I found it difficult to yell through my sore throat the following day.

While Grandpa Joe bore the brunt of her rants, she rarely yelled at any of us kids, save for Joseph. She and Grandpa Joe raised Joseph since he was little, even before I was born. I think she tried to not play favorites among her grandchildren, but she always had a difficult time watching us gang up on Joseph, something we did most any time we got the chance. She often came to his defense, insisting we stop picking on him. I think she thought of him more as a son, rather than a grandson.

Every once in a while, Grandpa Joe would counter her yelling with some of his own. But most of the time, he simply got up and walked out the door. He usually walked the full three and a half miles to the greenhouse. I think the hour-plus-long walk helped him, because by the time he reached the greenhouse, he usually had forgotten about her tirades. He concentrated on all the work that needed to be done.

A hard-working, soft-spoken, and generally tranquil man, he sought peace and quiet. However, he lived in a world full of noise and chaos. If he wasn't fleeing the rage of his frantic wife, he was trying to grasp the actions of his abusive and wildly unpredictable daughter, who I, until tonight, thought was the meanest person on the entire planet.

He tried to talk to us kids about my mother, but he often found himself struggling to find the right words. As time passed, he gave up trying, reflecting, instead, on how he and Granny raised her. "I wish I wouldn't have given in every time she wanted something," he bemoaned.

I think he finally concluded that no matter how he raised her, she was simply not cut out for motherhood. "Nothing against you boys," he said. "I'm glad she had you, but she and Bill should have stopped at Joseph. Your mom and dad weren't aware of everything it took in parenting even one child. There's no way in hell she can take care of eight!"

When conflict arose, his daughter was often the reason for it. From time to time, she would start a fight, just to see where her father's loyalties lay. She had a very difficult time accepting that she didn't have absolute, unbridled support from her father on all matters. She once called him "a useless, pathetic old geezer who showed more loyalty to his goddamned plants than to his own flesh and blood."

Although old and growing frail, he did all he could to make his grandkids' lives a little more bearable. He said he believed we kids needed to get away from the turmoil, if only for a little while. He took at least one of us to the greenhouse with him every day. He reasoned the tranquility of the greenhouse provided us with some measure of peace and quiet. And while poor by any measureable standard, he always scraped enough money together to buy an ice cream or a candy bar for anyone working with him on any given day.

From the way I hear he's been talking lately, I don't think it will be too long before he goes to Heaven. I hear he lies on his makeshift bed after putting in a hard day's work at the greenhouse, and prays for Saint Peter to call him home.

Last time I talked to my father, he said he visited the greenhouse, and Grandpa Joe looked very frail. He also said Grandpa Joe warned against anyone mourning his passing, declaring that he would forever haunt anyone at his funeral not dancing for joy.

Though I know my brothers would sorely miss his calming presence, I'm comforted by the thought that if I don't make it through tonight, someone I know will soon be in Heaven with me. I am especially comforted it will be the practical, reasoned Grandpa Joe.

When his time does come, I wonder if his daughter, Feenie, will even bother to come to his funeral. I am a bit torn about that prospect. I understand she would have the right – some would even say *obligation* – to pay her final respects, but I find that a bit hypocritical. Perhaps instead of *final*, she could pay her *only* respects. God knows she paid little, if any, to him in the past.

I know I should not be calling Feenie anything other than *Mom*. However, I, Eddie, Jeff, and James have all not called her by that title ever since James physically fought with her, about two years ago. James said she didn't deserve the title, just like our father didn't deserve the title *Dad*, because a dad is supposed to protect his children. He declared "that damned geezer ain't ever done a damned thing to protect any of us."

Don't misunderstand me – I've never been foolish enough to address either of them as such. An encounter like that would have, in no way, worked to my benefit. When addressing them directly, calling either of them anything other than what they deemed appropriate would have likely found me in need of immediate medical help. However, when we kids discuss things amongst ourselves, we always refer to them as *Feenie* and *The Old Man*.

Feenie left us for the final time a little over a year and a half ago. I don't recall the exact day, but it was sometime before Halloween. When I arrived home from school that day, James and Eddie were rejoicing like never before. "Bitch is gone for good," James said, high-fiving Eddie in celebration, accidentally knocking him over his schoolbooks.

They said they celebrated when they got home to find she wasn't there. They rejoiced even more when they looked around to find she took all of her prized possessions with her. They couldn't contain themselves when Eddie read aloud the card she left for The Old Man. Poor geezer probably still doesn't know we read it, and we knew why she left.

She had left many times before, but never took her cherished belongings with her. She usually packed some clothes, maybe six or seven changes. On those occasions, she usually came back within a week or two. But that day, she took the silver dollar clock she won at Bingo, some of The Old Man's Avon collection, all of her jewelry, and her best clothes, including her expensive black fur coat.

In the months leading to their big fight, James argued with Feenie almost every day. In fact, he displayed hostility toward her ever since he was nine years old. He didn't like how she treated him or his brothers. And as soon as he grew big enough to where she didn't physically intimidate him, he always stood his ground.

Where she saw defiance, his six brothers saw heroism. When she beat me or any of my other brothers, as she did often, she always made us scream. But she either couldn't hurt James, or he refused to give her the satisfaction of knowing she could hurt him. The last time he cried after she beat him, he was eight, when she hit him with a battery strap across the back five good times. After wincing and finally letting out a bit of a whimper, he turned and promised her he would never cry for her again. She quickly hit him four more times on his butt and legs, but he didn't cry.

From that moment on, no matter how hard or how many times she lashed into him, he never changed his expression. Once in a while, when she would literally exhaust herself whipping him, he would frustrate her, turning to say "are you finished?" She would whip him a bit more, but could not break him.

Even though they are now in State custody, I think most of my brothers are happy she is no longer part of our lives. Donnie and Tim are too young to fully grasp all that has happened, so I can't speak for them. Though Eddie talks a lot about the future of the family, that future never includes Feenie. James might be a bit disappointed he didn't get one final showdown with her, but he is content with a Feenie-free future.

One could say her leaving for good set in motion the events that led to my unfortunate situation. But should I not be able to escape death's grip, I hope my brothers won't look back with regret. In the end, we all got what we desperately wanted for many years: Feenie out of our lives.

I don't even know where some of my brothers are right now. I hear Jeff is somewhere in Parsons with the same family he's been with for almost a year and a half. I think Donnie is in a similar situation up in Dailey. I'm not sure what has happened with Tim. Though I assume Joseph is still with Granny, I don't give a shit about where he is, nor do I care about what will happen to him.

James is in limbo right now. He is staying with his friends. He hasn't adjusted well to foster care. He'll be ok if he finds a family with lots of patience and understanding. He has proven a difficult challenge, preferring to stand toe-to-toe with foster parents who feel the need to impose their will on him. That approach has long proven futile. After all, his own parents could not affect his behavior by going that route.

Lee is troubled. Left to his own devices, he will probably do something on impulse, posing danger to himself or others. He has always presented some sort of enigma, displaying bizarre behavior at the most inopportune times. Having been put in the State Children's Home, he has yet to be placed with a family. I pray the family doesn't abandon him. He will need our help and guidance later on in life.

Finally I come to Eddie. Although he is still very young, I wouldn't call him naïve. My closest brother, he views all people and all circumstances with initial skepticism. He rarely lets his guard down, preferring to study his surroundings for indications of malicious intent. He is reluctant to warm to new families quickly. While helpful for negotiating a cruel world, that trait can also be detrimental in finding a good home. To some, his unwillingness to quickly reciprocate affection is equated with inability to do so.

Eddie and I have been talking a lot on the phone lately, mostly reminiscing about growing up in that old, dilapidated shack deep in the hollow. We've been comparing all the foster families we've been placed with over the past year. We've also been talking a lot about how our lives may have been different if either Feenie or The Old Man gave a damn.

I never even imagined the possibility I might not get to see Eddie in person again. It's been three weeks since I last saw him. Mrs. Kroy, the child welfare woman, took me over to visit him at the White's house, where he's been living for about two months now. They seem like pretty nice people, but I think their age will prevent them from taking him in for very long. He's already been in four foster homes, just like me. James holds the record, seven.

Eddie cried the last time we saw each other. He really wants the family to get back together. Standing in the living room of his foster family's home, and with both Mr. and Mrs. White within eight feet of him, he declared "Mike, we're never gonna be a family again, you know that. I'm sick of these foster homes. I'm sick of these stupid two hour visits. This life stinks."

Of course, I want the family back together, too. But truth be told, I really don't expect that to happen. I hate to admit it, but I think Mrs. Kroy is right. The Old Man simply cannot parent seven boys while working two jobs. I doubt he owns the skills needed, even if work is taken out of the equation.

Nonetheless, I couldn't allow Eddie to give up all hope. After all, it was usually he who came to my aid in the past. "I know it sucks, but if you can hang in there, we can make it back together," I told him. "The Old Man needs to do some things the State wants done before we can live together. I think he wants us together, but that evil witch, Mrs. Kroy, and the State are in charge of us now."

Still, if someone would have asked Eddie his preference – a life with Feenie or one without her, he would have chosen the latter. I would have considered it a tossup. I didn't like her, and my disdain for her grew stronger by the day. But I despised being in foster care, away from my brothers, just as much. Of course, if I had a crystal ball and could have foreseen today's events, then without question I would have chosen the former.

In case I won't be able to escape my predicament, I want all my brothers to know how I feel. I'd like to thank them all for doing their parts to make life just a little more bearable. While sometimes life has seemed a cruel monster, combating it with the assistance of six like-minded brothers was far easier than tackling it alone. I'd also like to let Eddie to know I really liked talking with him the last several days on the telephone.

As you might imagine, my mind is racing. I have so much I need to say. It's a strange feeling. When you're young and healthy, you usually don't even *think* about the possibility of dying. You focus on other things, like playing baseball, or doing homework, or crawdad hunting. You simply don't prepare for moments like these. That being said, I hope you'll forgive me if I come across as disjointed.

First, I must say if He does decide to call me home, I am nervous about the prospect of meeting God. I simply haven't readied myself. I have been told over and over God knows every thing I have done, or even thought about doing, in my whole life. Judging by what Granny has told me over the past few years, I think He might be a little disappointed with me. Although I'm still quite young, I know I've done things that have disheartened Him.

I have never envisioned God as a vengeful being, like so many of the preachers would have me believe. But I don't believe everyone gets a free pass, either. That being said, I wish I knew what criteria He uses in deciding who He allows into Heaven. I think my age might offer me an advantage. In the past, when questions on that subject arose in church, there was some consensus that age twelve was the cutoff where one became responsible for managing his relationship with God.

Given that, I know there would be lots of kids up there. I personally know of two who have gone to meet God. Timmy Summers, who died last year in a car accident, will be there. Johnny Pratt, who I played with a lot at school, was pretty sick when God called him home. He spent his final three months in a lot of pain, unable to even get up out of his hospital bed. I know his mom and dad were hurt when he died, but I think they were relieved he was finally out of pain.

Granny, for her part, simply repeated what she heard in so many hard-line Southern Baptist sermons, saying "you must be born again, regardless of your age, to enter the Kingdom of Heaven."

I hope God would understand that I don't fully comprehend what being *born again* really means. I think it means getting baptized and accepting Jesus, though I can't imagine why getting dunked in a river here on Earth has anything to do with being able to live forever in Heaven.

My thoughts right now don't center on the day's events, though I do wonder in passing if I could have done something to alter them. Rather, they randomly alternate between some of the happiest, most distressing and bizarre times of my life. I take some comfort that they don't "flash before my eyes," something I've heard happens if one is truly at death's door. No, they show in remarkable detail, some as vividly as if I was experiencing them in the moment.

I can't imagine anyone as young as I capable of recalling so many and so varied, except maybe my brothers and, though I haven't seen him for a long time, Tony Waybright. I feel sorry for that poor kid. His brother seems to get just about anything he wants, often at Tony's expense. I don't think Tony gets enough to eat. I've witnessed him struggle needlessly through winters without good shoes and coats. And though he always seems happy on the outside, I can't help but wonder what he is feeling on the inside. He's a good friend, and I like him, but I don't think I would want to trade my life for his.

Chapter 2: The House and the Creek

I wouldn't consider myself an expert tradesman, but even a child with no formal training could tell the old shack wasn't constructed well. While most homes were built on solid foundations, the shack rested on twenty-nine stacks of cinder blocks. Five stacks were placed roughly six feet apart under each of five large wood beams spanning the length of the house. Four additional stacks, one at each corner and positioned perpendicular to the beams, provided extra support. Each stack consisted of three cinder blocks, with the bottom block forced beneath the surface.

Hard to believe maintaining a livable shack required such effort. When it came to making repairs, The Old Man constantly played catch up. Working two jobs, along with a hefty share of overtime, he did repairs when he had time, a rare commodity. Unless something posed a substantial risk of seriously injuring or killing one of the kids, the repair was usually done on Sunday or in the middle of the night, provided The Old Man didn't have to get up too early for work.

Once, however, he did have to take two whole days off work just to repair the floor. Lee had been bathing in the washtub one Sunday afternoon when it gave way, sending him and the washtub to the ground below. The Old Man and his friend, Old Man Waybright, reinforced that area with four-by-fours and two additional sheets of plywood.

I don't know why Feenie and The Old Man chose that place. Not only hazardous, it was far too small for nine people. Six boys crowded one bedroom, while Feenie and The Old Man slept in the other one, with the baby, Tim. The kitchen barely contained room for a four person table, let alone the oversized table and bench seats built by The Old Man. The living room held enough space for one large couch, which was usually occupied by either The Old Man or Feenie, or both, forcing the rest of us to sit on the floor.

As you might expect, we fought over sleeping arrangements. Not that it mattered much; we always ended up carving out a small space on the floor to sleep, only to wake in a different spot after getting kicked and pushed through the night. I often woke in the middle of the night to push someone's leg off of my face. Every once in a while, I woke to someone having rolled over on top of me, making it hard for me to breathe.

The shack sat in a clearing roughly two hundred yards deep by two hundred yards wide. The northern perimeter abutted Cheat Hill. Cows grazed in a field across the dirt road, to the south. All twelve in the herd belonged to the Grants, who lived up Ike Hill, to the west. Town, populated by four thousand, three hundred and thirty-seven residents, was about five miles east.

Making our way through the hollow to our house from the main road was tough work, even in perfect weather conditions. Travelling it in the wintertime, or after a heavy rain, was a nightmare. I can't begin to tell you how many times my brothers and I were called on to help push my parents' bogged-down cars out of the mud.

The hollow was much like many others in the country. Turning left off Cravensdale Road, approximately one hundred yards of paved road gave way to about a half mile of gravel. Gravel faded, leaving only a dirt road for the remaining mile or so.

Thousands of trees rose from both sides of the road. Their branches stretched across the road, intertwining with branches of trees on the opposite side. Summertime saw leaves so plentiful the sun never hit the dirt road directly beneath them. Those same leaves prevented summertime rains from drenching the road and making it unable to travel.

Halfway between the end of the gravel and our shack, a gate, comprised of four pieces of guardrail running horizontally welded to two vertical metal posts, stretched across the road. If the dirt road was in good condition, Feenie and The Old Man drove their cars through the gate, all the way to the house. Otherwise, they parked in an area near the end of the gravel and walked the half mile or so to the house.

Working the gate was tough work for us kids. Sure, The Old Man could easily open it, pull the car through, and close it in a matter of seconds. However, if there were kids in the car, they were tasked with operating it. We struggled to open and close it, knowing both The Old Man and Feenie had very little patience for us.

We were usually given thirty seconds to jump out of the car, unlock the pin, and swing the gate across the road. We got another thirty to close it, lock it, and get back into the car before the yelling began. Frustrated at our inability to work it quickly, Feenie often just drove off, leaving us to walk. The Old Man, on the other hand, usually yelled a bit, called us "little pussies" and various other names until we made it back to the car.

That gate was more than just a device to keep the Grants' cows from escaping. Those living on the east side of the gate deemed themselves somehow more civilized than the three families living to the west of it. We on the west were *hillbillies,* while those to the east were *town folk.*

I never understood why people shunned that label. I liked the people on our side of the gate. We didn't pretend to be something we were not. While I'll admit the manner in which we conducted our lives suggested nothing other than the hillbilly label placed on us, those who lived to the east lived no differently. In fact, most everyone I knew lived precisely as we did, the sole exceptions being the many foreign students that attended the local college. I've always believed that if one is born and raised in Appalachia, then she is, by definition, a hillbilly.

A small, two bedroom, neatly-kept shack stood in a clearing between the gate and our house. Feenie despised the lady who occupied it. I don't know what happened to make Feenie hate Rose Martin, and I'm not sure if *nemesis* is the correct word to use, but the mere mention of Rose's name would trigger an outburst. They rarely spoke, but when they did, it almost always escalated into yelling, screaming, and name calling.

I think Feenie was a bit jealous of Rose. She made no secret of her disdain for Rose's various states of dress, or undress, depending on whose point of view one was looking from. When Feenie saw Rose in a bathing suit, which she did often in the summertime, she always made it a goal to point out any flaw in Rose's appearance. She once commented to Rose that she should "learn to keep her hedges trimmed." I didn't know what trimming hedges had to do with Rose wearing a bathing suit, but the comment set off a heated argument.

Feenie often accused Rose and The Old Man of doing stuff behind her back. Once, when The Old Man drove too slowly past Rose's house, Feenie ran to meet him before he even got out of the car, slapping at him while screaming "why don't you and that slut just get it over with." I wasn't sure what *it* was, but Feenie often

16

made *it* a subject of first conversation when The Old Man got home.

I often thought Feenie and Rose would end up physically fighting. I don't know how that would have turned out. Feenie was small, probably weighing no more than one hundred and ten pounds. Though Rose was taller and heavier, what Feenie lacked in size, she made up for in temperament.

Rose's two daughters could be found playing outside on most days. I heard them say their real names once, but I don't remember what they were. I came to know them simply as "Tink and Sis." Or, if Eddie spent too much time talking with them, "Stink and Piss."

Far from town, the shack didn't have electricity. We burned enough candles to give us sufficient light for doing homework and our nighttime chores. One was usually left burning on the kitchen sink at night, offering just enough light to make it to and from the outhouse. Not that it mattered much. As far as I know, all of the kids peed off the back porch if they absolutely felt the need in the middle of the night. I suspected The Old Man did, too. If Feenie felt the urge, she had the convenience of a store-bought toilet, the sort that children learned to potty train on. She must have used it often, judging by how frequently she carried it out across the road in the morning, rinsing it out with a half bucket of water.

A traditional, country, coal and wood stove provided heat, at least for the front living room and the adjacent bedroom where The Old Man and Feenie slept. Heat never reached the back bedroom, where all that separated the rest of us from the elements was a plywood wall covered with tar paper. Trust me, when it's bitterly cold outside, it's brutally cold inside a room devoid of insulation and heat.

That said, wintertime drove the six kids from the back bedroom and into the living room. Seeing our breath as we tried to sleep provided clear indication it was time to move to a warmer area. We all managed to somehow find space on the living room floor, close to the wood stove.

When we did sleep near the stove, we made sure we had two buckets of water on hand, in case an ember popped out of the stove and started a fire. We knew something like that was a possibility, but when weighed against the very real prospect of freezing to death in the back bedroom, we elected to take our chances. While water was plentiful, it took a lot of effort to recover. It had to be drawn from the well, roughly thirty yards north of the house. As wells go, it was unremarkable in appearance, nothing more than a deep hole in the ground. Cold, clear water rose from the bottom, some twenty-five feet down, to within six feet of the surface. Covering the well was a big, brown concrete, circular construct. Slightly larger in diameter than the hole, it rose about three-and-a-half feet above the ground.

I hated that well. At first I hated it because it scared the hell out of me, having claimed far too many buckets and pans. From the time I was given the assignment of bringing in each day's water, I hated it because it stole so much of my time and energy. I especially hated it during the winter months, when its near-freezing water splashed all over me, adding to the misery of being out in the bitter cold.

Technique was required in recovering water. A cooking pot was secured to a y-shaped rope, made from strips of bed sheets, tied around its handles. If thrown correctly, meaning the pan hit the water open-end first and at the proper angle, water would begin to fill in. Otherwise, it just sat on top of the water, requiring it to be lifted completely out of the well and tossed down again. I must have made a hundred attempts before I recovered my first full pot.

When Eddie got big enough, he was assigned to help collect the day's water. Although it took him way too many tries before he finally mastered the technique, I was happy to have the help, especially during canning season and on weekends, when laundry and bathing required a seemingly endless supply.

The kitchen stove struggled to keep up during those times, sometimes operating non-stop for up to sixteen hours each day. Its fuel, flowing in from two large propane tanks sitting directly outside the kitchen window, could deplete in less than a week.

The Old Man warned the kids about staying away from the propane tanks. He placed them on a big, flat rock slab. He drilled out two holes into the side of the house to route the gas lines. Since the holes were slightly larger than the pipes that ran through them, we packed newspaper into the holes to keep air and bugs out. Surprisingly, it worked pretty well.

Bathing progressed slowly, as did laundry. In the winter, we added several five-gallon buckets of heated water to several buckets of cold water, until a lukewarm mixture was reached. While suitable, perhaps even preferable, for laundry, it never seemed to provide the necessary warmth for a relaxing bath. Perhaps that was precisely the point. Feenie wanted the process to resemble an efficient assembly line. We needed to get in, get clean, and get out as quickly as possible.

Summer often found us bathing in the creek. Formed by runoff from the mountains to the north and west, the creek flowed north to south across the property, and its cool water provided for refreshing baths during the summer. Provided the creek wasn't muddied by recent rains, The Old Man bathed five or six times a week, saying he preferred a complete body wash to the washrag and bucket of warm water that awaited his nightly arrival home. However, wintertime always found us bathing in the large metal wash tub on Sunday.

Behind the house, we added a wood porch, which we used as storage for the wash tub, as well as all of the gardening tools. The garden lay directly behind the house, running a hundred yards or so deep. Every available kid spent the bulk of each spring day preparing that garden for planting. We hoed and weeded part of it every day during the summer. When we reached the end, we started back at the beginning the following day.

Late in the summer, just before school started, we spent entire days harvesting vegetables, husking corn, or just getting the necessary water. We also spent a lot of time helping Feenie can food for the upcoming winter. I hated canning season. Each step in the process had to be performed in exacting detail. Harvested fruits and vegetables had to be cooked to perfection. Only adequately boiled water could be used to sanitize jars and lids. The combination of glass jars, boiling water, and what she deemed as reckless kids always seemed to test her patience to the core. She had canned every year since I was a baby. And every year, jars broke. The only variable in that equation was which child was deemed responsible for breaking a jar, and jars seemed as precious to her as water was to fish.

We built a little wood shed about fifty yards from the outhouse, to the northeast. When we killed a deer, which we did often, we took it into the shed, where we gutted and skinned it. Skinning deer was hard work, especially in bitterly cold weather. I can't count the number of times I feared losing my hands to frostbite.

At least when it was cold, the shed was easier to clean. On warmer days, we gagged from the horrific stench of deer guts. Sure, the outhouse reeked in warm weather, but it was a different smell. I don't know if people are naturally programmed to tolerate that smell or if we had just become immune to its affects through frequent use, but it never made me gag.

Once we finished, we carried the tub full of entrails, head, and damaged meat through the garden and dumped them over the fence at the rear, into a ditch covered in thick vegetation. I don't know what happened out there on the other side of the fence, but most of what we dumped was usually gone by morning.

Summertime was clearly my favorite time of year. Each day, when Eddie and I finished bringing in the day's water and hoeing the garden, we played. We sometimes could be found in the middle of the dirt road, pretending to be famous baseball players, while hitting little mounds of hardened dirt with sticks. At other times, we could be spotted catching bees or fishing worms.

Sometimes we set out to catch snakes, but they were harder to find than bees or worms. More often than not, we came back in the late afternoon empty handed. Some of those otherwise unproductive days turned out to be the best, with Eddie and me just talking about life as we saw it.

Country life might seem boring to a lot of people, but I never wanted summer to end. Whenever school resumed in autumn, teachers asked us what we did over the summer. Most of the kids described vacations and different places they saw. Every year, I had the same story to tell. It usually started with "I spent most of my summer with my brother…"

Living so far up in the hollow, I didn't have any friends my age, nor did I need any. Sure, when school resumed, I talked to and played with other kids. But as long I had Eddie and as long as water flowed in the creek, I was happy.

Eddie and I spent the better part of nearly every summer day in the creek. I'm uncertain if it was catching crawdads I enjoyed so, or if was simply spending my summer days relaxing and talking freely with Eddie. Either way, the best days of my life were spent on the creek.

Thick brush covered the creek in the summertime, making for some tough going. We would often travel with a sickle in hand, stopping to cut through vegetation we were unable to cross. We'd sometimes cut it just to make sure we didn't get bitten by any big spiders that might be lying in wait. It slowed us down, but on the creek, we were never in a big hurry anyway.

Life seemed somehow easier when we were in the creek. The farther up we traveled, the less we thought about Feenie. We could let our guards down, not living in fear that our next move might trigger an angry outburst.

While we walked on eggshells all the time around her, she didn't seem to be quite as cruel when The Old Man was home. We fell into the routine of doing our chores early, then spending the bulk of each day avoiding her as much as we could. We usually came back home late after we thought The Old Man was back from work.

While his presence helped ease our fears that she might do something so drastic she would leave us permanently injured or worse, there were occasions when even when he was around, she was as mean as if he wasn't there. Take, for example, the time she caught me picking my nose:

Chapter 3:   Don't Pick

Five of us kids were loaded up in Chrysler with Feenie and The Old Man. Jeff was in front with Feenie and The Old Man, while Lee, Eddie, James, and I were stacked in the back seat. The car didn't have air conditioning. July heat and humidity added to our collective misery.

We had been driving up and down almost every street in the whole town. Feenie and The Old Man used to cruise the town looking for couches that people threw out when they purchased new furniture. Hence, the shack's living room played host to a different sofa each year. Before it was allowed inside, we kids would have to scrub it down and let it sit outside for two or three days so it could air out.

I was bored. "Eddie and I could have been out in the creek," I thought. I hoped The Old Man would either find a good couch soon, or give up on the search until the following weekend. I asked "when can we go home?"

Feenie was just about to yell something at me. She adjusted the rear view mirror so she could get a better view of me. She got a better view, alright. I had my right index finger in my nose and I was twisting it around. I don't remember any pressing need to have my finger up there. Nothing of any significance needed to be picked out. I just had a habit of picking my nose, especially when I was bored.

She pulled her shoe off, climbed over the seat and cracked me on top of the head with the heel. I threw my hands up immediately to fend her off. The top of my head throbbed in pain. She smacked me about the head and face five or six times with the heel. Eddie pleaded with her to stop, while James demanded she do so.

She stuck her finger to my nose and poked it, screaming "how many times have I told you if I caught you doing that, worms would come out of your nose? HOW MANY?"

I had picked my nose hundreds of times before, and never once did I see a worm come out. I knew she was just trying to scare me, but I also knew I had better answer her question, or I'd get it again with the shoe. "A lot," I said, still rubbing the top of my head.

"You're damned right, a lot!" she yelled. "So why in the hell do you keep doing it? Huh? ANSWER ME! Why do you keep picking that stupid little beak of yours when I tell you to stop the shit?"

She paused and stared. The car grew silent, each of my brothers awaiting my answer. Nervous anticipation filled the air when any one of us got in trouble, especially when it boiled down to a kid-versus-Feenie confrontation. We all understood that the severity of the punishment directly correlated to the answer given.

She developed a two part procedure to instill and keep discipline in the family. First, she gave the offender a severe beating. Following the beating, she meted out a "teach-you-and-your-brothers-a-lesson" punishment. The beating was a guarantee, and it came courtesy of whatever object she could find nearby that would inflict the most pain in the shortest time. Her "lesson" punishment, when she had time to implement it, was often worse.

"I don't know," I said, continuing to try to rub out some of the pain from the knot forming on top of my head.

She yelled back angrily "you better give me a better explanation than 'I don't know.' And you have thirty seconds to do it. The clock starts now. I'm waiting."

I glanced over at my brothers, hoping one of them could help conjure up an answer that would make the impending punishment less severe. Each was trying to come up with something – anything – to ease the tension. Unfortunately, thirty seconds meant exactly that – thirty seconds. It may have meant slightly less, but it never meant one second more, especially when she was as angry as she was then. Time had run out.

Furious, she asked again "well, why do you constantly pick your nose when I tell you not to?"

I timidly offered nothing better than "I don't know."

"'I don't know' is all used up. It's been laid to rest. I know, because I personally killed it and buried it yesterday," she shouted. "Rules say you can't use an excuse that I already killed. Pretty soon, there aren't going to be any left for any of you little bastards to use."

She told The Old Man to stop the car at the nearest dumpster. I had no idea what she was planning, but I was relieved when the dumpster we pulled up next to was completely empty.

Undeterred, she ordered him to find another. She was determined to teach me a lesson, shouting "I don't care if we have to drive to every dumpster in this whole damned town; you're going to stop picking your nose." Stupid Sunday afternoon! If it was any other day, she likely wouldn't have had enough time to see it through.

We stopped at the dumpster behind Duke's. It had a few boxes and some garbage, but she decided against that one. All the while, I continued to wonder what she was planning. I thought "was she going to put me in a dumpster and make me live there?" If so, I figured I'd just get out once they drove away.

Next, we went to the one behind the Tygart Hotel. I was thrilled to see that one empty. It sat in an alley, where no cars ever came through. I didn't know why, but she wasn't quite as menacing when there were lots of cars or people around. James later said it was because "she didn't want the whole town to know what a psychotic bitch she really was."

> I wish I knew what was going on inside The Old Man's brain. He had to know how deeply she terrified us at times. And he had proven on occasion he was both willing and able to stop her. Every once in a while, when she would beat on Lee badly, he would immediately put a halt to it. Once, when he came home and found her still beating Lee with switches even though Lee's legs were bleeding, he told tell her to sit down and calm down, or he would put those same switches to her ass.

My brothers were growing anxious as we made our way from dumpster to dumpster. James told both Feenie and The Old Man to "give it up. The whole damned town is against both of you. They emptied all the dumpsters, knowing you two psychos would try something."

I knew he was trying to deflect their collective anger onto him, as he often did in those situations. In the midst of heightened tensions, he frequently said things so offensive he left my parents no choice but to immediately focus their anger toward him. While his rants often absolved the original offender of punishment, he often found himself condemned to harsher punishment than the original offender would have received.

That particular afternoon, they remained undaunted. Though James continued to hurl insults at both of them, they just continued on, seeking a dumpster that met her exacting requirements. I was amazed they were able to restrain themselves.

We stopped at one behind the Kwikstop. It, too, was full of mostly empty cardboard boxes. The one behind Hedrick's tavern was filled with boxes and empty beer cans. The one behind the Five and Dime had only boxes. Though she seemed to like what she saw at the one behind Scottie's, with the city park packed full of people, all potential witnesses, they decided against that.

All in all, twelve dumpsters had been inspected and turned down for one reason or another. I began to believe that no matter how hard they searched, they would be unable to find the one to satisfy her needs. "Perhaps someone up there was looking out for me," I thought, staring at the roof of the car, but envisioning the open sky.

Unfortunately, my elation was short-lived. They finally found one that she seemed to be happy with, behind Wilfong's Market. She told The Old Man to park the car. Wilfong's was closed, like most businesses were. Again, stupid Sunday afternoon!

Reaching through the rolled down window of the rear door on the driver's side, she grabbed me by my ears. I resisted, but I think she would have gone so far as to physically pull my ears completely off of my head. In pain, I allowed myself to be pulled to the door. She threatened to jerk me through the window by my ears if I didn't get out. Not wanting to suffer a life without ears, I complied. She told the rest of the kids to get out of the car.

I snickered to myself as she tried in vain to lift the metal lid of the dumpster. While she had no problem

27

opening the lid, her slight frame – all four feet and eleven inches of it – didn't allow her to get it all the way up until it flipped over so it rested against the back of the dumpster. After three unsuccessful attempts, she yelled at The Old Man "Bill, get this goddamned lid up now."

After The Old Man rushed over and did as commanded, she began sorting through heaps of nasty garbage. Worry quickly began to overtake me as I witnessed her sorting through it. Though she wasn't averse to getting dirty, she had, in the past, avoided it when possible.

She finally found what she had been looking for. Resting near the top of the dumpster was some old chicken in a half-open foam container. It gave off a horrible stench, but I could handle it. I had smelled stuff that nasty before. Try cleaning up deer guts on a warm November day, and you'll understand I could stomach pretty much anything that dumpster had to offer.

I thought she was going to make me take a good whiff of the rotten meat to teach me my lesson. I felt a little relieved inside. I figured I'd put on a little act, letting her believe I was sickened by the smell. I reckoned I might even gag a time or two to sell it.

"No," I thought, "the show will have to be more impressive since there are several of us together. Simply making me sniff some rotten meat's not all she's gonna do." All the kids had smelled worse stuff than what was in that dumpster.

A sobering silence filled the air as she stared at me. She seemed to enjoy the moments leading up to the actual punishment. Jeff said it was "psycho time, a time when she gets to play her mind games." I have to say it was effective that day. While James would have met her stare with an equally uncompromising glare, I glanced away.

28

I caught a glimpse of the chicken. Infested with what must have been a million maggots, I silently hoped she wasn't going to make me eat these gooey, crawling larvae. Sure, I had eaten worms and insects before, but I did it on my terms. If I lost a biggest crawdad contest to Eddie, I might have had to eat a fishing worm. But the terms were agreed upon beforehand.

"Grab some," she screamed, pointing to the maggots.

"How many?" I asked, already fairly certain of the amount that would be needed.

"Grab a handful of maggots now, you little son-of-a-bitch!"

I reached in and grabbed a handful. I tried to stay away from those still on, and in, the chicken skin, figuring the chicken itself was rotten. I showed them to her. Still not knowing what she had planned, I began to cry. "Is this enough?" I asked.

Without answering, she said "now put 'em in your nose."

Eddie was crying, begging her not to make me do it. James was no longer just mildly upset, he was growing furious. He turned to The Old Man and shouted "Geezer, you seriously going to put up with this shit?"

Feenie shouted to James "you'd better shut the fuck up, or I'll have Bill put a belt to your ass."

"Your time is comin', woman!" James shouted back, moving out of arm's length away from The Old Man. Little doubt ever entered our minds where The Old Man's loyalties lay on matters regarding Feenie's disciplinary measures. If she demanded it, he would have beaten any of us to a bloody pulp. She had the final say, period.

Surprisingly, she paid little attention to James. Instead, she focused on delivering the punishment she set out to deliver a short time earlier. She shouted at me "I said put 'em in your nose, NOW!"

Knowing I'd immediately get pummeled if I didn't do as told, I quickly shoved the whole handful into my face. I held my mouth and eyes closed until those that didn't make it into my nose fell off my face. A couple made their way into each nostril. I cried "I can't breathe!"

She quickly responded "if you can talk, then you can breathe. You best leave them there until I tell you to blow your nose."

She lectured my brothers, declaring that they were witnessing what was to be the unchallenged punishment for anyone she caught picking his nose from that moment forward. Though vividly illustrated by the events occurring directly in front of them, if I was in any of their shoes, I would have found the lecture a bit hypocritical. The Old Man picked his nose at will. Not only that, he wiped it anywhere he damned well pleased. And I don't remember her once lecturing him about it.

After about ten seconds, I started to gag. When I felt one of the maggots attempting to make its way into my brain, I immediately blew snot and maggots out of my nose.

James grew even angrier, and began making physical threats against her. She could still take him, but it was getting harder by the day. He was solid, built like an oak tree. He worked from the time he was seven, loading flour into vats down at the bakery. Ironically, the backbreaking job she made him work to bring in more Bingo money prepared him physically for the eventual showdown that changed the family dynamic forever.

She took off her shoe and whacked me across the face. Thankfully, the toe end struck me. "Did I tell you to blow? Get another handful, put them up your nose, and so help me, if you blow them out before I tell you, I will beat you to death!"

I grabbed another handful. Knowing the blow-maggots-get-smacked cycle would continue until I did as I was instructed, I had to think of a way to get through it.

"Wait," I thought. "I could do it if I imagined they were rice." I had put a few pieces in my nose before, and felt no ill effects. In fact, I remembered once challenging Eddie to a "how-many-grains-can-we-put-up-our-noses" contest, which I won, thank you very much, with thirteen pieces to his meager ten.

With that in mind, I pushed another handful to my face, careful not to open my mouth until all, except those that went into my nose, fell off. I just kept thinking "it's just rice, nothing wrong with that." I managed to keep them in, but my eyes watered.

"Stop your damned cryin, NOW!" she screamed, standing directly over me. Though she still towered over me and all of her younger children, I knew there would come a day when I would outgrow her. James was almost there already.

James yelled everything he could think of to distract her. Although he was doing his best to deflect her attention towards him, I think it would have probably have been better for me if he had just let her finish her punishment.

She turned again to my brothers and shouted "you little bastards want to look like this, just let me see you pickin' your stupid little beaks!"

After thirty seconds passed, she allowed me to blow them out. "Next time, they stay in there all day! You understand?"

Crying, I replied "yes ma'am."

I wondered how long it would be until she caught me again. After all, she tried in vain to make Eddie quit chewing on his shirts. She beat him mercilessly. She cut holes in his shirts and made him wear them to school.

She soaked them in vinegar. Once, she cut up a shirt, soaked it in soapy water, and made him chew it until he puked. All that, and still today he chews on his shirts.

As soon as we got back in the car, she took off her shoe. I braced for another beating, so I quickly curled up in the fetal position. But she smacked James across the face with it, screaming "you better never talk to me like that again, boy! I promise it'll be the last time. AM I CLEAR?"

James did not answer.

"I SAID, AM I CLEAR?"

Still no answer.

She smacked him again across the face with the shoe. "Answer me, you little bastard!"

He just sat there staring at her...*through* her. I think she sensed James would not answer her, no matter how many times she hit him. She put her shoe on and told The Old Man to drop her off at Granny's house for a bit.

After she got out of the car, James glared at The Old Man. He said "grow a set of balls, Geezer. I'm telling you now that I won't take much more of her shit. One of these days she's going to lay a hand on me, and I'm going to mess her up! Won't be long off, either. Fact, if you weren't in the car just now, I would have smashed her face in"

The Old Man quickly countered "and that will be the day you die, because I'll choke the life out of you with my bare hands."

"Don't matter," said James, "at least I'm going to bust her up before I go."

The Old Man quickly grew annoyed, declaring "that's enough shit for one day. I can only handle so much shit, and I have reached my fuckin' limit. Now, I don't want to hear another goddamned peep out of any of you!"

Sensing the anger in his voice, we all remained quiet for the rest of the ride home. Once we got there,

The Old Man told Jeff to look after us. He left and went back toward town, to get Feenie.

Eddie asked me how I was doing. I told him I was ok. He said "Mike, we can't let this go. That wasn't right. Parents shouldn't treat their kids like she does. James is pissed off. He'd probably beat her up in the morning when The Old Man goes to work, but you know when he gets like this, The Old Man won't let him stay here. So it's gonna just be us and Lee. We should do something!"

The following day, after we brought in the water and hoed the garden, Eddie and I hit the creek for a few hours. We made our way back home late that afternoon. Feenie was getting ready for Bingo, so we stayed in the back bedroom until she was about ready to leave. She barked a few orders, then left.

Chapter 4: Bees

Later that night, when Feenie got home from Bingo, she came into the bedroom, yelling. Before we knew what was going on, she jerked Eddie and me up out of bed. I wasn't fully awake when the pain from the battery strap slamming against my legs registered. Through my crying, I asked her "what did we do?"

Although she beat us far more than we felt we deserved, I assumed she had a reason, at least in her mind, to merit a beating. Although there were countless times when we had no idea what we did, or might have done, to trigger an angry outburst, she insisted that if we listened, did precisely as we were told, and kept "our damned mouths shut," she wouldn't have to beat us. She liked to cite that old axiom "children should be seen and not heard."

She shouted "I told you two to fill the wash tub so Lee could wash the clothes."

I really didn't remember her telling us to do that, but she insisted she told us earlier, before she went to Bingo. I thought "funny, Lee doesn't remember her telling him to wash clothes, either." He got his beating before she jerked us out of bed. He was still sniveling, even as Eddie and I were winding down our loud wailing.

Experience had already taught us that talking back on Bingo nights, especially those nights when she was not in a good mood, was met with a swift and decisive pummeling. That said, we complied with her orders.

I'm not sure what happened to put her in such a foul mood on those nights, but I often wondered why she continued to do something she knew would upset her. I'd like to think if I wasn't forced into something that upset me, I'd just simply quit doing it.

She made us bring in eight, five-gallon buckets full of water. Eddie was hurting much more than I. She had cracked him across the ribs with the battery strap. I had welts on my legs and butt, but he had one on his back and one on his side, right up under his rib cage, and it was slowly turning purple.

We helped Lee wash. Lee and I alternated, each scrubbing two or three pieces, then resting a bit as the other scrubbed. I didn't realize washing clothes on a washboard required so much effort. By the time we finished, my shoulders hurt bad. After that night, I felt even sorrier for Lee. Eddie and I grew sore after a few hours in the garden, but scrubbing clothes on a washboard for hours on end gave me both a whole new level and a whole different kind of soreness. I would have liked to soak in a hot tub, but that would have required much more labor.

After washing four large piles, we brought another six buckets in for rinsing. Rinsing was far easier than washing. We simply placed the soapy clothes into the tub, filled it with water, pushed on them a bit, then pulled them out.

We finished the clothes at about two o'clock in the morning. Eddie and I stayed outside talking with Lee, as he hung them onto the clothesline. It was dark, but he was pretty good at it. Neither Eddie nor I were tall enough to reach the clothesline, so we handed the clothes to Lee, and he pinned them to the clothesline, one piece at a time.

When morning came, I was surprised Eddie woke up at his usual time. He had two big mason jars in hand. I didn't know precisely what he had planned, but I figured it had to do with the beating we received on the previous night.

Feenie was still too big for Eddie and me to fight. We knew if we tried to physically confront her, she would beat us silly. But, while she had a considerable advantage in size and strength, we had nature on our side.

Explorers that we were, we took no issue with nature. Feenie, however, loathed it. Bees, snakes and spiders all terrified her, to the point that she had Jeff and The Old Man put up a screen around the front porch to keep the insects out.

We held that nature was solely responsible for providing us with nourishment, and we treated it accordingly. When we gathered, we were careful to leave enough berries and apples to provide for the animals. When we hunted, we made every effort to kill quickly. I had seen documentaries in school about the importance of not making animals suffer, if possible. I agreed with that philosophy.

The Old Man was always working at one job or another, so Old Man Waybright taught us how to hunt. A hillbilly in every sense of the word, Waybright could truly live off the land. He almost had to. He never finished the fifth grade, having been driven away by the merciless teasing he endured for being Albino. Fortunately, society had progressed a bit, and his two albino children endured far less teasing than their father did.

Since we were still very young, Eddie and I could only use the .22. The older kids got to use the .270 or the .30-.30. James and Jeff could handle the 12 gauge. They hunted squirrel and groundhog and rabbit. Eddie and I looked for turkey. We wouldn't shoot at anything with the .22 unless it was stationary.

It was yet another warm summer day, a perfect day to be in the creek hunting crawdads. Unfortunately, crawdads did not serve the needs of that day. Feenie's brutal beating with the battery strap the previous night rendered breathing difficult for Eddie. He gasped and wheezed uncomfortably doing the simplest of physical activity.

Eddie's bruise had grown substantially overnight. It completely covered his bottom two ribs. He was pissed off, not only for the beating, but for the whole maggot incident too. Needless to say, I was also a bit worked up. James was working, so it was up to us to do something.

Two large apple trees stood prominently along the southern perimeter of the field where the cows grazed. A few weeks earlier, we noticed a whole nest of yellow jackets in the center of one tree, right where the branches and trunk met. We didn't go in the field often, figuring since the cows didn't give us any problems, we shouldn't give them any. Once in a while, Tink and Sis wandered about in there, but only to explore.

Eddie's condition made it hard to get over the gate. I hopped back over and pushed him up. We walked through the field, staying about twenty yards away from the seven cows grazing near the fence along the dirt road. They either didn't notice, or they didn't care, that we were on their turf.

As we walked toward the apple trees, we called Feenie every name a seven and eight year old kid could think of. "Cow poop eater," Eddie wheezed. "Stinky rat-face witch!" I exclaimed. Eddie tried to laugh, but I could see it caused him a great deal of pain.

We were careful around bees. We had caught many of them in the past. We had also experienced the pain and misery that came with not affording them the proper respect. Eddie had been stung at least ten times the previous year and I probably got it twenty times. I usually got stung about once every five days or so in the summertime. It always hurt like hell, but fortunately, the pain didn't last too long.

We arrived at the tree with a purpose. I never asked Eddie what he thought the limit should be on how many times he could be stung. I was willing to collect as many bees as I needed, no matter what the cost. Eddie had an equally determined look.

At least a hundred wasps crawled around on many of the damaged apples that had fallen from the tree. I didn't know if they were eating them or drinking the juice, but they seemed to be content. They didn't even get stirred up enough to chase us off.

Seeing that, we thought it would be a good idea to put a piece of an apple in each jar. Eddie smashed an apple on a rock. Ample amounts of juice dripped from it. He gave me half to put in my jar and he put the other half in his jar. We then went about collecting bees.

Eddie caught one, then quickly covered the jar with the lid. "Easy as pie," he said as he screwed the lid down onto the jar. We had stabbed holes in the lids earlier to make sure the bees could breathe.

They didn't even seem to notice they were getting caught and being held captive. Once inside the jars, they all just went to the apples at the bottom of the jars and crawled around on them. We managed to get pretty close to the hive without getting stung even once. I thought about just scooping up a whole bunch right from the hive, but figured it was probably too risky.

After collecting about forty or so, we headed back down the field, toward the house. I think Eddie might have been having second thoughts, judging by his trembling voice. "She's going to get real mad. Even if she doesn't get stung once, you know how she hates bugs."

I agreed with him, but the plan had already been set in motion. By rule, a plan set in motion could not be stopped, unless it posed immediate risk of serious harm or death to a participant (Feenie excluded). Sure, she

38

would be mad enough to make that a reality. However, if I had a well-thought-out escape plan, then risk of serious harm, while prevalent, wasn't immediate.

If we could get a thirty yard head start on her, we knew she could never catch us, especially in the creek. We had run through that creek nearly every summer day for the previous two years. We knew everything about the creek. We knew where the unexpected holes were, which rocks were easiest to slip on, and any other possible pitfalls. The creek was a strategic ally. It was *our* territory.

I told Eddie to go to the creek and get ready to run. He needed a bit more of a head start that day. He again asked if I was certain I wanted to go through with it. "If she catches us, she'll beat us. I can't handle another one today," he said, pointing to the dark purple bruise covering the bottom portion of the left side of his rib cage.

"I promise she can't catch us," I said. "Can you run?"

He jogged about ten steps. Grimacing, he turned and said "I think so, but not like yesterday. I can't swing my arms very well."

I told him to go up the creek about another hundred yards. "She won't even be able to see you," I promised. I don't ever remember her coming up the creek more than thirty or forty yards.

I walked with him a ways up the creek. After we agreed he was at a safe distance, I said "ok, you stay here. Give me your bees."

We knew that if the plan failed, there would be hell to pay. We also knew that if the plan was only moderately successful, meaning she only got stung a few times, there still would be hell to pay. I hoped we had enough to sting her to death, but deep down, I fully expected her to survive. I didn't even really expect she'd have to go to the hospital.

No matter. I was going to let them loose in her room, and let the chips fall where they may. I planned to mete out some measure of justice for the beating she gave us the previous night. Eddie's ribs demanded she pay.

When I got to the house, I expected her to be up and about. As I approached, I saw Lee in the kitchen, cleaning dishes. He glanced down at the jars. I put my finger to my lips, gesturing for him to be quiet. I whispered "where's Mom?"

Lee was broken, both physically and mentally. Grandpa Joe used to say he was a different kid when he was younger, but all the beatings had broken his spirit. "She's trying to turn him into the daughter she never had," he said.

I hadn't known any other Lee than the quiet, timid one tasked with doing virtually all the inside chores. He was the third oldest, but James, the fourth oldest, was much stronger in every way, except running.

Indeed, Feenie demanded nothing short of perfection from Lee. Clothes and dishes had to be spotless. The shack had to be kept clean, an impossible task, given so many kids making messes. Most importantly, he had to remain at the ready to give Feenie anything she wanted. He didn't get outside to play very much.

Grandpa Joe said "Thank God she didn't have the medical know-how or she would have given him a pussy." I didn't know what he meant until later on, when I asked James. Gross!

"She's still in bed," he whispered back. Looking back down at the jars, he began to understand the purpose of the question. He quietly ran out the back door, leaving it open for me. Lee didn't need the creek to get away. He ran cross-country for the junior high team. He could run for miles, never seeming to tire. Feenie could never catch him if he was outside. For that matter, I don't think The Old Man could, either.

I pulled back the blanket covering the doorway to her room just enough to peek inside. She was still sleeping. Standing there all alone, I thought for a moment about not going through with it. I thought that if she caught me before I got away, she would literally beat me to death. Fortunately, my fear was fleeting. I was doing it for my brother.

I shook both jars until the bees got mad. Buzzing angrily, they wanted out of the jars. I knew I would be stung many times if I just unscrewed the lids and let them fly. "There is only one way," I thought. "I have to lob them into the air in her room. When the jars hit the hard floor, they will break and the angry bees will take her down."

Again I peeled back the blanket. With one jar in each hand, I tossed them into the air towards the corner closest to her face. As I ran out of the house, I heard the glass break. I didn't look back as I raced for the creek. I heard screaming. "Good," I thought, as I sprinted across the yard. "I hope they make her pay."

I made it to the creek and ducked down. Staying low, I looked back to see if she had seen me. Thankfully, she hadn't. She must have been too busy dealing with the bees. In all the commotion, I remember hearing four distinct screams.

Careful not to make any noise, I slowly crawled through the creek bed, forty or so yards, to where Eddie was. Well-hidden behind a tangled maze of thick brush, we watched her run from the house, out into the garden, screaming. I was happy she was getting her just desserts.

"You bastards!" she yelled, studying her surroundings for clues as to who could have done it. As soon as she began to turn to look in our direction, Eddie and I lay flat in the creek.

As she continued to survey her surroundings, we peeked up over the bank to catch a glimpse of her. I didn't know where Lee was, but I figured he ran up the mountain, towards the Grants. Wherever he was, I sensed he, too, was watching.

After ten fruitless minutes of screaming and yelling for us to "get our asses back to the house," she relented and went back inside. We watched from the safety of the concealing brush as she chased bees out of the house with the broom. I'm certain she killed all those that elected not to leave when prompted.

Still pretty early, Eddie was upset she was able to get away. He said she would just wait and beat us silly when we got home. We decided that staying away for the day would be best.

We played in the creek all day. We found some blackberries. In the early afternoon, we slipped undetected into the garden and picked some tomatoes, washing them in the creek. They tasted bitter, but we surely did not want to go back to the house.

Evening came quickly. We hoped it was Bingo night. As we made our way toward the house, we saw The Old Man's car. We were relieved the blue Chrysler was nowhere to be found.

Once inside, Eddie took his shirt off. He reasoned that if The Old Man saw the bruises on his ribs, he wouldn't allow her to beat him about the torso when she got back. The Old Man was lying down on the couch. Eddie walked past him, making sure he saw the condition she left him in the previous night. The Old Man had been in bed asleep the previous night when

Feenie pulled us up out of bed and beat us. He saw Eddie's bruises, but he never said a word.

James came home a short time later. He usually brought home any extra bread from the bakery that didn't get sold while still fresh, but they sold everything they made that day. Ms. Schmidt, the bakery owner, gave him a gallon jug of peanut butter. Seeing that, Lee ran for the spoon, while Eddie got a loaf of bread.

When James saw Eddie's ribs, he blurted "that stupid bitch needs to die!" Then he looked at The Old Man and said "look, if you don't want us, tell us. We'll build a place over in the other field. This shit's got to stop. If you won't stop it, I swear I'm going to gut the bitch."

The Old Man yelled "I don't want to hear your shit tonight, boy. I know it's gotta stop, but goddamn it, you boys deserve to have your asses beat once in a while."

James went over, got Eddie by the arm, and took him to within about two feet in front of The Old Man. He shouted "you tellin' me a seven year old kid needs this shit? Is her pussy that good that you'd let her kill your fuckin' kids? You're a dumbass."

The Old Man jumped up and backhanded James, knocking him to the floor. Standing over James, he shouted "I said I don't want your shit tonight!"

James remained defiant. As soon as The Old Man walked away, he jumped to his feet and shouted back "The hell with this. I'm going to bring the cops back home tomorrow night after work. Maybe they'll do something."

The Old Man grew more agitated. "I said that's enough. You bring the cops out here, and I'll beat you to death myself! Now, you'd best get your ass to bed, or you're going to get hurt."

James stared at The Old Man for about ten seconds, testing his patience.

"MOVE!" shouted The Old Man, his patience clearly having worn thin.

I sense The Old Man knew there was too much violence, but I think he hated the thought of confronting Feenie about it.

Sensing The Old Man was ready to explode, James slowly trudged away.

We ate our sandwiches and went to bed. Expecting that Feenie would come in and yank us out of bed in the middle of the night, Eddie and I put on two extra pairs of underwear. James taught us that trick, saying "it works pretty well, providing she beats your asses and uses a belt, but it ain't gonna help if she gets a hold of a battery strap. That still hurts like hell."

I don't know what happened that night, but she never came in. We were both surprised and relieved when we woke up the next morning. Eddie was feeling a lot better, taking in full breaths again. We hoed the garden for about two hours, then went down to the creek, spending the bulk of the day catching crawdads.

Chapter 5: The Indian

Eddie and I headed to the creek earlier than usual on that July morning. The Old Man told us it was going to be very hot, so we began hoeing the garden at first light, each working non-stop for three grueling hours or so. We had already brought in the day's necessary water on the previous night.

Before Feenie came out of her room, we each ate one peanut butter sandwich and wrapped another in foil, to be eaten later in the day in the event we would be unable to locate something a bit more palatable. We bid farewell to Lee, who was sitting on the couch, awaiting the day's first demand of him. He remained at the ready, knowing he would soon be required to make Feenie her morning coffee as soon as she woke up.

As we made our way across the yard toward the creek, we stopped for a bit, playing in the hole Jeff and The Old Man were digging for the new outhouse. I didn't understand the need for even making a new hole. The outhouse wasn't yet even halfway full. Nevertheless, they had already dug a pretty impressive hole, perhaps three feet wide and long, and about two feet deep. They had been working on it, as time allowed, for close to a whole week. I figured they had to go a little more than twice as deep as they had already dug in order to copy the one in use, though I wasn't about to jump into the old one to confirm my guess. I wondered a bit about how long the new one would last. The one we had been using had been used by all of us for several years.

After finding eight fishing worms, we made our way to the creek, then began our routine trip north. As was custom, we kept every crawdad we caught at first, then replaced the smaller ones in favor of larger ones caught later on. The trip progressed slowly, but I didn't mind. Time away from Feenie was welcome anytime. It was necessary when The Old Man wasn't home.

We gradually made our way up to our usual turnaround point, about a mile up. The sun still hadn't reached its high, so we decided to keep going, figuring as long as we stayed in the creek, we could never get lost. We reasoned that as long as the creek didn't branch off, we could go as far as we wanted. We could simply turn around anytime we desired and follow the creek back toward the house.

We travelled farther up than we had ever gone before. We both hoped we wouldn't encounter a bear or a large cat, both of which had been known to inhabit the deep woods. Though we had never encountered a bear before, I always heard that no matter how fast we ran, we couldn't outrun one. I didn't want to have to try. We both knew that trying to outrun a bobcat or a panther would be an exercise in futility.

Continuing on, we examined the surrounding area for possible getaways. Small, sturdy trees were everywhere, and we were both pretty good at climbing them. So, about every fifty yards, we stopped to identify a tree we would use to get away from a bear. We also decided to arm ourselves with a couple of the many durable, sharp sticks that lay near the creek bank. While we knew we couldn't defeat a bear, we figured we might be able to smack or stab a bobcat, forcing it to run away.

Every now and again, we managed to catch a big, blue crawdad. It is still unclear to me how those gained their prestigious positions in crawdad hierarchy. Though no formal proclamation was ever drawn up, we deemed them more valuable than ordinary crawdads, akin to royalty amongst peasants in medieval times. While I personally never held them in as high regard as Eddie did, I liked to catch them for their bartering value. Sometimes Eddie offered two big regular crawdads for just one blue one of equal size. I usually traded with him. Heck, on a trip lasting as long as that one did, we always caught six or seven of them anyway, so I always got to keep one or two for myself.

We worked our way up toward a bend that began a slow climb. The sun was approaching its afternoon high, indicating time was closing in for us to begin our journey home. But since our buckets were already nearly full, we knew our trip back down would go much faster than it did upstream, so we decided we would turn around and head back down after we reached the bend.

Along the banks, we found wild grapes and blackberries, both of which seemed to be in greater supply the further we travelled. Eddie collected a fair share of both, while I stood guard for animals that might have wanted their share. Looking back now, I realize how small each of us would have looked to a big black bear foraging for those same berries and grapes. Thank God we didn't have a chance encounter with one.

Strange, but we generally ate well in the summer, supplementing our three peanut butter and jelly sandwich diet with apples, wild grapes, blackberries, and the occasional tomato stolen from the garden. I'm ashamed to have to admit it, but neither I nor Eddie told our brothers of all the fruit we found, though they knew of the apple trees over in the field.

If I knew how to keep those damned mosquitoes, bobcats, bears and the like away, I would have preferred to just live in the woods during the summer. But while animals were fun to look at in the daytime from a distance, I didn't want to meet up with one in the middle of the night.

By the time we made it to the bend, we both had plenty of crawdads in our buckets. At that point, the trip wasn't so much about catching crawdads as it was just exploring. We still looked for crawdads, hoping to find that ever elusive lobster-sized one. We just didn't hunt for them as vigorously as we did when we began our journey.

I had just picked up a long, flat, shale-like rock, letting the flow of the creek naturally wash away the murky water. Once it became clear enough to see, I nodded, providing indication to Eddie that a nice, fairly large one was there, waiting to be caught and placed in one of the buckets containing the day's catch. He was good at crawdad hunting. I was still better, but he was good. Years of experience allowed us to perfect the art. Our instincts allowed us to position ourselves to give us the best chance of catching them.

I was a bit surprised Eddie didn't move in immediately after I informed him of our potential prize. After all, that was the way we had done it for three years running. I can remember only one other time when he didn't follow that routine. One day the previous summer, he stepped on a jagged rock and folded into the middle of the creek, needing a full seven minutes to recover.

I looked over to see what was taking him so long. His face was drained. He was as pale as a ghost. He stood there frozen, staring intently at something behind me.

The hair on the back of my neck stood on end. Never before had I seen the look that covered his face. His big eyes were open wide. His mouth was tightly closed, and his nostrils flared with each rapid breath he inhaled.

I whispered "Eddie, what is it?"

He didn't answer. He couldn't.

I imagined a bobcat or a bear was standing directly behind me, ready to pounce. I slowly bent down and filled my hand with the cool creek water. Careful not to make any sudden movements, I flicked the water onto him. He didn't as much as blink when it hit his face.

He glanced at me, then immediately redirected his attention on what was behind me. "Eddie, what is it?" I whispered again, pleading with him to answer me.

He glanced back at me and said "Indian."

I flung down the rock I was holding. I immediately began running back toward the house. All I knew about Indians was that they liked to cut people's scalps off. In many of the Westerns on the TV at Granny's house, which The Old Man and Grandpa Joe watched with equal passion, Indians were always killing people. I didn't want to become one of them.

I sprinted right past Eddie, giving little consideration to the jagged rocks protruding the creek bed. It may have meant spending the rest of the summer rehabilitating a punctured foot or a broken ankle, but I figured a foot injury was a far better option than being scalped and slow-roasted over a fire.

I must have run a full fifty yards before I realized there was no sound of splashing water behind me. "Why hadn't Eddie followed my instruction?" I thought. Any reasonable person easily would have done what I did: run as fast and as far as humanly possible.

Attempting to make an abrupt halt in order to turn and see what was happening, I slipped on a slimy, moss-covered rock. As my legs went out from under me, I flung my arms down to cushion my fall. My hands didn't touch water before my hip slammed against that same rock.

Writhing in pain and rolling around in the middle of the creek, I managed to catch a glimpse of Eddie. He stood there, still completely motionless. Though I was a bit disappointed he hadn't turned to see how badly I was hurt, I was relieved he was still alive.

The intense pain in my left hip began to dissipate. As I pushed myself up, my eyes caught what his was focused on. Clad in leather, a large, brown-skinned Indian stood roughly ten feet from the creek, arms folded, staring at my brother. Unlike the television shows, however, he didn't have paint on his face, nor was he chanting. In fact, he remained completely silent as he stood.

"Eddie, run!" I screamed, imagining the Indian was only moments away from grabbing him and taking him home to eat. But Eddie didn't move.

I was torn. I wanted to run all the way back home and get the .22. Though I had only killed two living things with it, I never had once thought about having to use it on another human. I certainly didn't want to have to use it, but I think I would have found myself capable, if I truly believed he was going to kill us and eat us.

"No," I thought. "I had to stay and fight, even if that meant getting killed and eaten along with my brother." Eddie had never abandoned me. He always reasoned things out in a way that seemed to make sense. I didn't know how to make sense of that moment, why he wasn't running for his life. But somehow he just knew who and what were dangerous, and what people's intentions were. He stayed, so I stayed.

For about two whole minutes, as I stood in the middle of the creek rubbing my hip, they just stared at each other. I stared at the Indian man, hoping he found us too little to make a decent meal of. I hoped his tribe had some kind of code or something that declared kids couldn't be scalped until the age of fifteen or so.

I have no idea what was going through each of their minds. I quickly imagined many and varied possible scenarios. Unfortunately, none ended with either me or Eddie making it home alive.

Eddie picked up his bucket of crawdads and made his way up the creek towards the Indian, about twenty yards away. He sat the bucket down near the Indian's feet. The Indian remained stationary, arms folded, silent.

Eddie untied the small plastic bag full of berries and grapes from around a belt loop of his cut-off corduroy shorts. He opened it and offered its contents to the Indian, asking him if he was hungry. The Indian stood there, motionless.

Eddie sat the bag on the ground, then offered the Indian his whole bucket of crawdads. I thought "are you crazy? Grapes and berries are one thing, but crawdads are precious cargo, not to be given away on a whim."

The Indian slowly unfolded his arms. I feared Eddie's time was up. I ran to help my brother, screaming for the Indian man not to hurt him. Instead, he reached for the bag of berries on the ground and picked it up. He handed it back to Eddie and said something that to me sounded like "what the hell are you doing here?" or maybe "get the hell off of my land!"

I was more than happy to oblige. Eddie, however, wasn't the "let's-leave-this-guy-alone" kind. He was curious. He wanted to know where the Indian came from, where his kids were, what he ate...everything. Given the chance, he would probably even try to get the Indian to invite him over to meet his family.

Eddie took a handful of grapes out of the bag and went to the creek and washed them. He took them back to the Indian, who opened his massive hand and accepted Eddie's offering. He slowly raised one to his mouth, intently staring at us. Looking back, he must have been just as amazed at seeing us as we were of him. He ate all five grapes Eddie gave him.

I slowly and cautiously made my way to within ten feet of both of them. Eddie's face glowed. He was as happy as I had ever seen him. He took the whole bag of grapes and berries to the creek and washed them, then returned to give them to the Indian. The Indian took the grapes, then reached into the inside his leather jacket. Pulling out two turkey feathers, he gave Eddie one.

He laid the other feather on the ground, motioning for me to come and get it. He backed up three steps as I approached and picked it up. I grinned widely, my toothless mouth displaying my age.

He never spoke a single word, but he did not have to. He knew he had just made two children very happy.

Eddie and I spent the next thirty minutes gesturing to the Indian. The Indian man made us feel welcome. From the moment he placed the feather on the ground, I never once felt uncomfortable in his presence.

A short while later, the Indian pointed to the mountain up creek. I think he was attempting to tell us he lived further north, somewhere in the mountain, and was expected home. In unison, Eddie and I pointed towards our house, down creek.

We took our feathers, held them high, and smiled at him. We nodded and thanked him for his gift. He nodded back, took the bag of grapes and berries and headed up creek. We took our feathers and crawdads and headed down creek, back toward the house.

I can't be certain, but I think the Indian considered us his friends. I know I never feared another Indian from that moment forward. I didn't believe anything I saw in any of those Westerns The Old Man and Grandpa Joe watched later on.

By the time we made it home, it was early evening, about six o'clock or so. I don't even remember walking home. Eddie and I spent the entire trip back down the creek just talking about the Indian. "I bet he knew how to start a fire. We should have asked him to show us," I said.

Suddenly we were within one hundred yards of home. As we approached the house, we heard Feenie screaming at Lee. We didn't know what she was screaming about, but assumed it was probably something petty. Perhaps Lee put a glass on the cup shelf while drying and stacking the dishes. Or maybe he missed a spot of jelly when he wiped off the kitchen table. We didn't always understand why, but Lee got yelled at a lot.

We decided it best not to tell Feenie about our encounter. We reasoned that she'd probably demand The Old Man take a few of his work buddies hunting up in that area, and to not come back without Indian hide. Evil witch!

As I lay here, I wonder if I'll ever see the quiet, friendly Indian man again. I hope he knows he provided us one very memorable afternoon in the summer of nineteen seventy-three.

Chapter 6: Joseph

On those summer days when Jeff worked at the YMCA and my parents wanted to go somewhere, They dropped us off at Granny's. I usually didn't mind. After all, Granny lived in town, close to the high school and its well-maintained baseball field, where Eddie and I used to climb the fence to play, using whatever we could find to make it as realistic as possible. Feenie and The Old Man went to the fair to see some singer named Conway Twitty. Both she and The Old Man thoroughly enjoyed listening to country music. The mere mention of any other genre, save for maybe bluegrass, initiated heated arguments. Both James and Jeff knew that, and often used it to rile them up. One time, Jeff went so far as to say "no country act should ever even be allowed back into an arena where Led Zeppelin played. I'm gonna write the President and ask him to make a law."

Eddie was working with Grandpa Joe at the greenhouse. Since it was Saturday, Lee had to stay at the house and do laundry. James was at the bakery, where he could be found hard at work on any Saturday. The only reason they took me there that day was to hoe Granny's garden.

Although she held a full sixty-four years of life experience, Granny was unskilled in reading people.

I'm unsure she even fathomed humans, with the exception of The Old Man, whom she blamed for never allowing her daughter to reach her full potential, capable of doing unmentionable evil. That said, she could do little to protect those in her care.

She had already raised a daughter who plainly didn't hold the tools to properly parent. Grandpa Joe admitted to that on numerous occasions. Granny could not bring herself to agree, however. She argued her daughter did everything she could to forge a better life for the kids. She did concede that her daughter simply had too many kids, too soon. "If she had spaced you boys out a little more, she would be able to better take care of you," she said.

While it is possible she may have actually believed it, I think it more likely she was just trying to convince herself. She must have known Feenie was deficient in matters of parenting. Why else would she and Grandpa Joe have taken Joseph at such an early age, unless maybe she herself wanted a second chance?

I knew little about Joseph, other than that he was my oldest brother. Whenever a group of us went over to visit Granny, Joseph certainly didn't act as though he was one of us. In fact, I submit that he didn't want to even be perceived as being one of us. Eddie said Joseph thought he was better than us because he had running water, electricity and a television. He called him a snob who "has his nose so far up Granny's butt, he can always tell what she ate for breakfast."

While Granny frequently drove Grandpa Joe away with her yelling and screaming, Grandpa Joe always firmly stood his ground when discussing how Joseph should be raised. He wasn't happy how Granny pampered Joseph. He once told her the last thing the world needed was a "male version of our selfish, poor excuse of a daughter," a remark which prompted an angry, profanity-laced response from Granny.

When she uttered profanities while screaming at him, he quickly remarked that people who resort to such language lacked an educated vocabulary. That only seemed to intensify her outrage, frustrating her to the point she eventually walked away, ranting under her breath. She clearly did not like any remark that questioned either her intelligence or how she talked. Since I didn't spend a great deal of time at her house, I can't speak to how Granny raised Joseph. But I was proud of Grandpa Joe when he fought back. I wish he had more energy, so he could have fought back more often on other topics. Work must have drained him, though. When he did finally make it home, he mostly just wanted some peace and quiet.

They lived in the upstairs part of an old two story, tar-shingled shack. The first floor of the place was filled with old gardening tools, like scythes, sickles, and old manual lawn mowers.

While an abundance of spiders kept the downstairs relatively free of insects, cockroaches could be found everywhere in their living quarters. During the evening, when I'd get up to get a glass of water, I'd see at least ten of them scatter when I turned on the light.

Separated from the living room by a semi-transparent lace curtain, her kitchen was very small. The refrigerator, two-burner stove, and two-seat table crowded the room. Back in the living room, a small yellow couch and a green reclining rocking chair filled it so it was difficult to walk without hitting one of them. An old television, used primarily for Westerns and on Saturday nights for Hee-Haw, sat on top of a little antique coffee table abutting the wall separating the living area from the tiny single bedroom, where Joseph slept.

Granny's eyes sometimes played tricks on her. I corrected her many times that day, reminding her I was Mike, not Eddie. Sometimes she got very confused. If three or four of us kids were at her house at once, she had a lot of trouble keeping track of us. She seemed to have more trouble in the afternoon. She called each of us by our correct name in the morning, but she seemed to become more confused as the day wore on.

That afternoon, Granny needed some sort of medication from the drug store. She said she'd be back in about an hour, maybe an hour and a half. I offered to run to the store for her, but she insisted the exercise would do her good. I understood, and watched her as she walked down the alley, slightly hunched over to the front and to the right.

After she disappeared from sight, I went about hoeing her garden. I hoed for about forty five minutes or so, then I started to get thirsty. I continued on for about another five minutes, ready to start on the tomatoes. I figured I had reached a good stopping point, so I ran upstairs to get a glass of water.

Joseph was watching television. I don't recall exactly what he was watching, but it was either "Bonanza" or "Ponderosa." Honestly, I couldn't tell them tell the difference between the two. I did, however know the characters "Festus" and "Sheriff James Arness" of "Gunsmoke."

At that time, I never really understood the appeal of television. Later, when I found out the Flintstones were on every day after school, I often invited myself over to the Gilbert's house, staying just long enough to catch them before running home. Eddie usually tagged along. He was in our grade, even though he was younger.

I had just got my water and was going back out towards the door, when I heard Joseph say "hey Mike, you want to see something cool?"

"Sure. What is it?"

He took me to his room and brought out a Rock-em-Sock-em robot. He then asked if I would like to have it. "Of course," I thought. What eight year old boy in the whole wide world wouldn't want one? Why would anyone even feel the need to ask that question? That was akin to asking Feenie if she would like a cigarette after four hours without one.

I said I would love to have one. But then I remembered Eddie. If I had one and he didn't, then we really couldn't have fun, could we? I believed if he was in my shoes, he would rather have none at all, than have only one. So I asked him "do you have one for Eddie?"

Joseph thought for a moment, then said "look, I really like these things a lot. But I guess I'd be willing to give them both to you if you'll try something."

I imagined I'd have to eat a cockroach or maybe clean the dishes to get them. "OK, but we got to make it quick. I need to get the tomatoes finished before Granny gets back."

Joseph sat down on the bed. He said his pee-pee hurt and he needed me to help him make it stop hurting. He pulled both his pants and his underwear down to his knees. He asked "can you put your hand around it and move it up and down? That helps it feel better."

I was confused. Never before had I ever been asked to touch another male like that. I didn't even like having to scratch The Old Man's back in the wintertime, when his skin got so dry countless flakes of dead skin would get under my nails, forcing me to scrub them with a hard brush until I could see through them again.

But Joseph pressed on. He promised me it wouldn't take long. Though I remained wary, I reluctantly agreed. Those two robots resting on the top of the bookcase begged to be played with.

He showed me how I was supposed to do it. It didn't look too difficult, so I quickly did as I instructed.

A very short time later, his wee-wee was standing straight up. Mine looked like that sometimes in the morning when I had to pee, so I told him "maybe you should go pee. That will make it go down again."

He said he would pee in a few minutes. He sat up, asking me to keep massaging. "That really helps it feel better." He said.

Another minute passed. "Mike," he said "you know when you get older, sometimes instead of pee, some other stuff comes out of your wee-wee. It makes all the pain go away, too, when it happens. It's white and tastes like ice cream. Can you help get it out?"

Eight years of life experience hadn't yet prepared me well enough to realize what he was doing. Thinking I was doing nothing more than helping a brother, I told him I would try to help.

"The problem is it can't come out unless you have my wee-wee in your mouth," he explained.

I had no idea what he was talking about.

"Come here, I'll show you," he said.

He put his index and middle fingers in his mouth, then bobbed his head up and down.

"Can you do that to my wee-wee? It'll only take a couple minutes, I promise." When I showed wariness, he persisted, saying "I wouldn't ask, but it's the only thing that helps make it feel better."

He still needed to pee, I thought. I hoped he didn't pee in my mouth. I closed my eyes and did to his wee-wee what he did to his fingers. After about two minutes, the white stuff came out.

I recoiled. It tasted nothing like ice cream. In fact, it tasted far worse than the saltwater I gargled with when I had a sore throat. I spit it out and ran to the kitchen to get some water to wash out the taste.

Eyes watering, I told him I didn't like it, any of it. He said it was ok. He said he was sure I would like it, but he was wrong. He said next time he would pull his wee-wee out of my mouth before the white stuff came out.

As he handed me the robots, he quietly said "you probably shouldn't tell anyone about this. You know how Dad sometimes flies off the handle before he gets the whole story. If he asks you where you got the robots, tell him that Granny gave them to you for doing such a good job on the garden. Otherwise, he'll think you stole them and he'll whip your ass."

Though he made a compelling case, I somehow felt he was trying to protect his own ass from a good beating. I remember only one time when The Old Man beat Joseph, but it was a beating of epic proportions, which is saying a lot, given how often he delivered them.

About ten months earlier, Grandpa Joe couldn't explain to The Old Man's satisfaction why he ended up in the hospital with two broken ribs. He told The Old Man he slipped and rolled down the stairs. While that seemed plausible, The Old Man pressed him. "I've never seen you once come down the stairs without holding the wood rails," he told him. "If you slipped, you would have dislocated your shoulder like you did when you slipped getting out of the bathtub. That little bastard pushed you, didn't he?" Grandpa Joe turned his eyes to the floor, saying nothing.

Though Granny was usually able to mediate, she knew by the force with which The Old Man stomped on the stairs there was little she could do to protect her favorite grandson that day. She could only watch as The Old Man dragged Joseph by the hair, out of her house and down the stairs. She pleaded for The Old Man not to hurt Joseph.

Once they reached the bottom, he slapped Joseph harder than I ever remember him hitting anyone, save for some of the men he caught Feenie running around town with on those occasions when she left for a couple weeks. Joseph wilted, bleeding from his mouth as he fell to the ground, crying.

Not yet satisfied, The Old Man was determined to get a point across. He informed Joseph his impending beating was going to be especially brutal, unless he told the truth. "I hear anything I think is a lie and every one of your pussy little teeth go flying across this garden, do you understand?"

Joseph admitted to pushing Grandpa Joe, causing him to fall. The reason? Grandpa Joe wouldn't give him money to buy an album he claimed he needed. With that, The Old Man slapped him hard again, his huge hand jarring Joseph's face, instantly knocking him back to the ground. He warned Joseph that if Grandpa Joe even so much as had a scratch on him from that day forward, Joseph would be "eating teeth three meals a day until there were none left."

The Old Man went on to say he'd be making daily visits to Grandpa Joe from that day forward. He told Joseph "if I even suspect you're thinking about picking on that poor old man, I will knock your ass so far into last week, you'll never get caught back up, you little son-of-a-bitch!"

Suffice to say, Grandpa Joe suffered no more suspicious accidents.

I took my two robots downstairs and placed them beside the house, before he changed his mind. I grabbed the hoe and began working the tomatoes. I couldn't shake the feeling I had just done something dirty. I began to feel ashamed.

As the afternoon wore on, I felt worse and worse. I stayed outside for the rest of the day. From that point on, if I needed food, I snuck over to Mrs. Winan's apple tree and took one or two. If I needed water, I used the hose Granny put out to water the garden. I just didn't feel like going back upstairs to be alone with Joseph.

When Granny finally made it home, I was happy to see her. I had just about finished the whole garden. Her garden was a lot smaller than ours. Three of us couldn't hoe our garden in three days, but I myself could finish hers in a few hours.

"I got you some suckers," she said as she reached into her store bag. She handed me an orange one and a red one. She asked me what I wanted for lunch. I told her a peanut butter sandwich would be fine.

After I finished the garden and lunch, I asked Granny if I could go home. There was still enough daylight left to easily make it home.

She said "your dad and mom won't be back for a couple of hours." Are you sure you want to walk all that way?"

I really didn't want to stay until Feenie and The Old Man came to get me. Besides, the bakery was on the way. If I wanted to, I could just wait for James to finish, and I would walk home with him. I just didn't want to be there with Joseph.

"Yeah. Besides, if it starts to get dark, I can always walk home with James," I said.

I made it all the way home with thirty minutes of daylight to spare. Lee had finished the clothes, and was enjoying a rare nap. James made it home just shortly after dusk. Eddie came home with Feenie and The Old Man about two and a half hours later.

As soon as Eddie and I were alone, I showed him the robots. When he asked where I got them, I told him what happened. "Joseph put his thing in my mouth."

He seemed perplexed. I don't think he understood, because he didn't have much to say about it, other than that it sounded gross. He wanted to talk about crawdad hunting we planned for the following day. He talked a lot about the funnies he read in the newspaper Grandpa Joe got him. He really liked Grandpa Joe.

Two weeks from that day, when Feenie went to drop me off again at Granny's, I cried and begged her not to.

"Please let me go to Bingo with you."

"Why? She asked. "Bingo is for adults. You wouldn't like it. Besides, Mom needs help working the garden. She might even pay you."

I was too ashamed to tell her why I didn't want to be with her mom. Looking back now, I wish I told her. I don't know if she would have believed me, and even if she did, I don't know if anything would have come of it. Granny would have done anything within her means to ensure her beloved Joseph wouldn't have had to pay too dearly.

I relived the entire scenario over again that Saturday. At least it was over quickly. I would have much rather Granny stayed home. But, wanting to get me some candy as payment for hoeing her garden, she had only gone to the KwikStop, a ten minute trip for me, but thirty minutes on her frail legs.

When I got home, I slammed both of those robots into the ground, over and over, until there they were unrecognizable. Sure, they were cool toys, but I paid far too steep a price for them.

The following Tuesday, I ran down to Mrs. Webster's house, about three quarters of a mile down the road. I told her I would be happy to help her son, Mark, hoe their garden on Saturday. They had a large garden, which meant more work, but work was better than being around Joseph.

When Feenie went to take me to Granny's the following Saturday, I told her I already promised to help Mrs. Webster. Though disappointed, she had little choice but to allow me to work Mrs. Webster's garden. I planned to spend every Saturday in that garden if I had to.

I know Joseph will not stop his deviant behavior on his own. I can only pray he gets caught or killed before he destroys somebody else's life.

If this is the night when God decides to call me home, I pray He will take into account how very young I was when I sold my soul for two stupid plastic toys.

Chapter 7: Hide and Seek

Eddie and I ate some strawberry cake sitting on the table. Always hungry, we knew that if we wanted cake, we'd better get it while we could. If we waited until the rest of the kids got home, we doubted we'd get any.

Lee came in and saw the half-eaten cake. He also saw Eddie and me with strawberry cake all over our hands and faces. He said "Mom spent the morning baking that cake for Dad for his birthday. You two had better get out of here. It won't be long until she gets back."

Though tearing through her homemade cake like wild animals provided immediate gratification, we quickly realized we had committed an unpardonable act. Things done in the past to merit a severe beating paled in comparison. We agreed she would beat us to death, or at least as close to death as the law allowed. We had taken beatings before, but we knew the one to come would be intolerable.

Eddie and I quickly determined there was only thing we could do: run away. Without so much as packing, we ran all the way to town, careful to stay far enough away from the main road she wouldn't be able to see us as she made her way back home.

Once we got to town, we searched for a good place to build our new house. I don't know how we came to agree upon the area behind Kroger, other than that it was familiar, and we knew they threw food out all the time.

Across the street from Kroger was a store that sold refrigerators. We needed only two of the large boxes they tossed out to make livable shelter. It took both of us to carry one, so we had to make two trips. Once we got them to our new home, we wrestled with them for over two hours, just to tear them apart. Who knew cardboard could be so dammed difficult to work with?

Kroger had heaps of little boxes. We used three to support the flaps converging at the center of our new home. Though I was ok with what we already had, Eddie said we'd be happy to have an extra layer, making the ground a little easier to sleep on. "Plus," he said, "crawling insects usually stay under the cardboard." That sounded reasonable, so I happily broke open enough boxes to cover the ground. I hoped nothing would bite us after we went to sleep.

We worried about Feenie. Once she realized we had run away, she'd surely have the whole town looking for us. We reasoned that she'd probably tell the police we beat up a baby, or stole a car; anything to turn up the heat and get the whole town looking for us.

We didn't expect a any problems on our first day away. While we knew we had run away, we didn't expect Feenie and The Old Man to know we were gone until very late in the day. We supposed they would think we were up the creek, catching crawdads, at least until it got dark. Only then, we reckoned, would they begin to think that maybe we weren't coming home that night.

As nighttime approached, we crawled into the makeshift house. A tiny glimmer of light came through a crack where the two flaps of our home overlapped. We were able to see well enough to make out each others faces. I don't know if Eddie knew it or not, but I was never fond of the dark. That said, having just that tiny amount completely eliminated any reason to be scared.

We lay there and just talked. He talked about Lee. He said he felt bad for Lee, because Feenie was always beating him. I told him "Lee's a lot older than us. She probably beats him a little harder because he can take it. She beats James a lot, too."

He replied "yeah, but she can't hurt James. He doesn't get hurt. I wish I had his muscles. I'd like to punch her back one good time."

As the night continued on, we talked about what we wanted to be when we grew up. I said "an astronaut. Those guys are famous since they went to the moon. I hope to get up there when I'm older. What do you want to do?"

He pondered for a bit, then answered "I'd like to try and help Lee. Not only Lee, but Tony Waybright. You see Tony? I don't think he's eaten anything in a week. Old Man Waybright gives Junior all the food, and Tony doesn't ever get anything."

I agreed with him about Lee and Tony, but I was hoping for a different answer. I asked again "what do you want to *be*?"

He thought for a minute, then said "I guess something to do with math. It comes kinda easy to me. I can understand the math that James has, and he's in fourth grade. I like science, too. Maybe I'll be a math or science teacher."

He opened one of the flaps that made the roof of our home, then continued on "or maybe I'll try and figure out how many stars there are in the sky. There are a whole lot of 'em. If you counted everyone by hand, they say you'd be dead, even before you counted the ones in our galaxy."

We got a little hungry. We sifted through the day's throwaways and found a box of powdered donuts. After eating two each, we decided to throw the other two away, feeling full.

We hadn't counted on how thirsty we would be after eating them. We needed water. We drank all the water we could from a hose in the front yard of the two story brick house, about fifty yards away. I know it's wrong to take without asking, but I hope the people who lived in that house will understand that since we were on the run, we couldn't chance it.

We made our way back into our house and talked until it was real late. I told Eddie "this has been the best day ever, next to the day we met the Indian."

He sighed and said "I think so too, but tomorrow's going to be even better. When we wake up, how about we head over to the park?

I thought that was the best idea yet. We used to drive past the park all the time. In all my time on earth, we had not once stopped to play in it. Every time we drove by, I saw tons of kids running around in the park, having loads of fun. I couldn't wait until morning, when I would finally get a chance at all those slides and the swings.

We talked for about another half hour. Eddie grew very tired. He had his eyes closed while I was talking to him. After a few more minutes, he quit answering my questions. He just fell asleep. I never saw Eddie fall asleep while talking. I decided to go to sleep too.

As I lay there looking at Eddie, I hoped he would make it to be a teacher. He did a lot of my math homework for me. He was already a grade ahead of his age. In math, he was in Mr. Hart's class.

I woke up the next morning to rain dripping on my head. The whole cardboard house was wet. I asked Eddie what we were going to do about the house.

"Plastic bags should do the trick," he said.

We both had to pee. We hadn't thought about that when we made our house plans. Daylight had arrived, and there were cars going up and down the street behind Kroger. I didn't want to go out in the rain to pee, so I got up on my knees and scooted up to the front opening of the boxes, which was about three feet from the back of the Kroger building. I pushed the door flap out of the way, and I peed out the opening.

Eddie must have thought it was a pretty good idea, because as soon as I finished, he went. Then he asked "what happens when we have to poop? We can't poop in the house. It'll stink up the place."

I thought about it for a while. "The park has bathrooms, don't they? We'll just make sure we go when we're at the park."

"Good idea," he said, handing me a dark banana. Like most every thing else Kroger threw away, it wasn't as fresh as we would have liked, but it was food.

We lay there and talked about the plan. At most, we would wait for an hour. Then we would go to the park, even if it was still raining. It seldom rained all day long in the summertime. If we were patient, we figured we would get our chance.

Skies began to clear shortly before eight, and we began our trek. The park was less than a half mile away. The Old Man was already off at work, and Feenie never got up that early, so we thought we were safe. Even so, we kept our eyes open for either the blue Chrysler or the brown Riviera.

We talked and played as we walked. We stopped and barked at a couple of dogs that barked at us as we passed their territory. After we mocked each other's barks, we pushed each other and talked about how we wished every night could be as good as the night we just spent.

When we got to about a hundred yards from the park, Eddie took off running. For a split second, I thought he spotted The Old Man or Feenie. Before I realized he was challenging me to yet another race, he had about a ten yard head start. He could run pretty fast, but I was more than a whole year older, and I could catch him. Although I needed the whole hundred yards to the park to pass him, I touched the slide a split second before he did.

The slide was still wet from the rain. I decided I wasn't going to wait for it to dry. The park had a lot of really big trees that kept the sun out. It would take at least two hours before they were completely dry.

I ran up the stairs and slid down, landing in a big mud puddle at the bottom. Forged by the feet of hundreds of happy children, it was a good two inches deep. I ran back up and slid down again. Eddie ran up and slid down. Back and forth, up and down, we rode the slide over and over again.

We ran to the merry go round. Nothing extravagant, it was made of six upside-down u-shaped bars welded to a metal platform. A well worn path encircled it, signifying it, too, was a favorite amongst kids.

Eddie pushed the go-round, running as fast as he could through the sloppy mud. I had tons of fun. I think Eddie did too. We pushed each other several times, but quickly grew tired. Pushing it was hard work, especially in the mud. Besides, Eddie was never much for just spinning in circles. He always exited feeling a little queasy.

Though they were considered *girly,* the swings were fun. We swung for about ten minutes, then we raced back to the slide. We alternated between the swings and the slide for the next two hours.

Later, while chasing each other, we found a Frisbee. Though we spent the better part of an hour trying, neither of us mastered tossing it like we saw other people do. Others made it look easy, flicking the disk so it glided like a bird through the air. When either of us tried, it didn't glide at all. It wobbled, then promptly dived, on edge, into the ground.

Sometime around noon, we decided to go back to our makeshift house to get some food. By the middle of that second day, we were growing adept at spotting blue and brown cars. Not yet skilled at identifying makes and models, we quickly ducked out of view whenever we spotted any blue or brown car that resembled the Chrysler or the Riviera. Sure, sometimes we had to make some last-second dives over hedges, or under parked cars, but we grew braver as time passed on. We were pretty sure we couldn't be caught.

After we ate some stale bread and a green bell pepper, we decided to head back up to the park. It was about two o'clock in the afternoon, a time when The Old Man was working and Feenie was usually putting on her face for Bingo. Almost two whole days passed without a beating. Our wounds were beginning to heal. We felt renewed. We very much enjoyed our time in the park earlier.

We were nervous as began our trek. We kept an alert eye out for either of the cars. As we made our way up Randolph Avenue, we passed the General Tire Company. The Old Man worked there sometimes on Saturdays, when he wasn't at the foundry. I'll give him this: he must have loved to work, because he sure did enough of it.

Eddie peeked in to the open bays at the General Tire. To our relief, The Old Man wasn't there.

We made it past a few home-based businesses. Then we passed the fancy church. I had never been inside that church, but judging by its outside beauty and elegance, I figured I had to be pretty rich in order to attend services there. I didn't figure I'd be attending anytime soon.

All that was left was the laundry mat and Scottie's, a restaurant famous in the area for their miniature burgers. The south perimeter of the park adjoined the road directly behind Scottie's. We would have the whole afternoon to play.

We planned to play until about five, when The Old Man got off work, unless he worked overtime. We would hide for about half an hour, then come back out and play until dark. After that, we would head back to our new home.

> Though meager by traditional standards, we felt the home was the best home ever. We enjoyed all the food we could eat. We didn't feel the sting of belts or battery straps or switches or high-heeled shoes. It was serviceable shelter for two young brothers trying to forge a new life.

We made it to the laundry mat. We stayed on alert for the Riviera and the Chrysler. We paid no attention to the little yellow VolksWagon Beetle that had just pulled into the laundry mat parking lot. That turned out to be a huge mistake.

Our light-hearted discussion about playing at the park came to an abrupt halt. Out of the blue, Eddie said "oh, crap! There's Dad."

I laughed, thinking he was trying to scare me. I turned to him to tell him to stop messing around, but from the look on his face, I could tell he was serious. I began to turn around, hoping to gauge how far away The Old Man was. Before I could get fully turned, the hulking brute grabbed me by the shirt. I knew I wouldn't be able to get away.

"Run!" I shouted to Eddie, hoping in my heart he wouldn't. I knew I was going to get it good. But somehow, a good beating was a bit easier to handle when Eddie was there. Following a beating, we would spend hours plotting our revenge. Plotting helped us take our minds off of our pain. Plus, it always gave us a reason to get up the next day.

Eddie yelled at The Old Man. "Why can't you just let us alone? We ain't hurtin' anyone. We got food and water. Plus, no one has smacked us around for two days now. Feels pretty good."

Eddie was about ten yards away. The Old Man shouted "Get your little ass in this car now, boy!"

Eddie didn't come.

"I SAID NOW!"

Eddie heard the anger in his voice. As he approached the car, he put his arms up over his head and waited to be slapped. But inexplicably, the slap never came. The Old Man grabbed him by the arm and firmly pushed him into the back seat.

As soon as he sat down in the front seat, The Old Man began to lecture us. Eddie tried to convince him to just leave us to live on the street. He told The Old Man "please let us live behind Kroger, at least until school starts. We'll come home on our own then, we promise."

I think he really believed he could talk The Old Man into it, but The Old Man wasn't having any of it.

My thoughts turned to the inevitable beating we would get when we got home.

The Old Man asked "why do you two always got to do things like this?"

Eddie quickly responded "because that's what we're supposed to do: run away from danger."

Startled, The Old Man quickly proclaimed "you two dumbasses don't know danger from your asses. The only danger you boys face is stepping on a snake when you're playing outside."

I thought "maybe he really is that blind. How could he see the all the bruises and welts all over our bodies, and not wonder how they got there? Maybe we should just walk around naked." I saw the big bruises and welts on Eddie almost everyday. I know he saw them on me. We both saw even bigger bruises and welts on Lee.

As we pulled into the front yard, we were relieved to see the blue Chrysler wasn't there. Jeff and Lee were washing clothes. The Old Man and Tom Higgins, the owner of the yellow Volkswagon beetle, went back to work to finish out their shifts. Jeff was told to not let us out of his sight.

Jeff told us Feenie and The Old Man had been looking for us almost all night. He said The Old Man didn't get to sleep until three in the morning, then woke up at five thirty to go to work.

We asked him how mad Feenie was. He said she seemed more concerned than mad. But he also said she'd be pissed off when she got home. "I think she's playing Bingo at the VFW tonight, so if you can stay out of her way when she gets home to get ready, then maybe she'll get over it and won't beat the shit out of you."

Lee needed more water from the well, so Eddie and I went and got it.

I don't know why we didn't get beat that night. Maybe Feenie had a real good night at Bingo, or maybe The Old Man told her he already beat our asses. Either way, I was pretty happy to see the sun come up, not having been dragged from bed and beaten through the night.

We spent the next several weeks working the garden.

Chapter 8: Free Fall

Canning season had come and gone, with little turmoil, at least for me. Lee spent much of the inside time working closely with Feenie, while Eddie and I did most of the harvesting. School opened as it always did, with the first few days a feeling out process. After a while, I settled into my routine.

The play area at Third Ward School was small, with a set of swings, some monkey bars and a little merry-go-round. The school sat up on a hill, about thirty yards above the main road. The school grounds sloped steeply down toward the main road, stopping abruptly at the forty-two inch high steel rails sticking up out of an eight foot concrete retaining wall. Looking over the rails, a sidewalk butted up to the bottom of the wall, separated from the main road by a set of guardrails.

The school itself was old, like much of the town. Desks had seen many generations of students travel through. Lockers, stacked two high, lined the walls. First through third graders used the lower set of lockers, while the upper set was used by fourth through sixth graders. Older students and younger students rarely ran into each other during the day. The older kids had to get their books and be in the classroom seven minutes before the younger kids. I figured the school created that policy to give the younger kids a chance to get their stuff out of their lockers free of torture from the older kids. At the end of the day, the young kids put their books back into their lockers and went to their busses seven minutes earlier than the older kids.

Snow fell the previous night. It usually didn't get so cold in late October, about once every four years. It wasn't much, just enough to cover the ground, maybe a half inch or so. A cold drizzle fell the day before, leaving the ground very slick. We promised Mrs. Poston we would be careful if she let us outside to play. She agreed, but reminded us the grass was slick and would be off limits. She took us outside and told us to stay in the recess area.

I was running through the recess area, reminding myself to stay off of the grass. When I rounded the building, I caught the edge of the grass. Before I could get back onto the sidewalk, I slipped and fell on my butt, then went sliding down the hill, toward the rails.

When I woke up in the hospital, The Old Man and Feenie were bed side. I hadn't yet become fully aware of my surroundings before I heard Feenie ask "why the hell were you playing so close to the rails?"

I didn't answer. I remembered falling and heading toward the rails, but I had no clue how I ended up in the hospital.

Doctors and nurses scurried about. One doctor shined a little light into my eyes, asking me a bunch of questions. Still not completely coherent, I was unable to answer them.

Over the next few minutes, I slowly began to regain my wits. I desperately wanted to get up and get out. Try as I might, I couldn't move. They had me tied down to the bed, with straps across my chest and my forehead. I could bend my arms at the elbow, but other than that, no matter how hard I struggled, I was locked in place.

I told the nurse I was ok and that I wanted to go home. The doctor explained that I needed stay still, because I had hurt my head. He said they couldn't fix it if I was moving. The Old Man, standing somewhere behind the doctors and out of my range of sight, declared "boy, you need to stay still so they can fix you."

I spent the whole afternoon and evening getting examined. I think they must have used ten different machines on me. They took X-rays of my head and neck. They shaved most of my head and hooked up a bunch of wires to it. I didn't understand what all the fuss was about. I didn't feel hurt, except for a little headache.

I guess I must have been unconscious for a while. I remembered nothing from the time shortly after I slipped until I woke up. I didn't remember Mrs. Poston jumping over the rail to attend to me. Likewise, I didn't remember the ambulance ride to the hospital. Nothing registered.

I spent the next week in the hospital, each day growing more and more restless. On the third day, my head started itching. When I reached up to scratch it, I felt the stitches they had put in to sew my scalp together. I had needed stitches before, but never more than the nine they sewed my shoulder up with when I fell out of the apple tree, landing awkwardly on the metal pot we used to collect apples.

Later, when Feenie came to visit, I asked her how many stitches I had. She said there was a hundred and twelve. She went on to explain that the stitches would come out in about ten days or so, but my skull had been cracked open and they did a lot of work to put it back together.

"The doctors say you're gonna have to take it slow for the next couple of months. You're gonna need to wear a protective helmet for a while, until your skull heals a little bit," she explained.

I thought about stupid I was going to look in a helmet. I knew my brothers would be ok with it, but other kids would probably make fun of me. Those same kids that poked fun at me and Eddie for being poor would have even more ammunition. I dreaded the thought, especially knowing I wouldn't be able to physically fight back for several months, at least until my head healed.

Feenie said the fall left me with something called epilepsy. She told me I might have unexpected seizures. Of course, I didn't understand any of the medical terminology she used, and I never gave it much thought. I was just looking forward to going home.

The doctors did their best to explain it terms I could understand. They insisted I needed to wear my helmet for the next few months, until my head healed. They impressed upon me the importance of taking my medication. Finally, they stressed that I would have to severely restrict most physical activity and completely forego anything involving heavy contact.

My arrival back home was met with apprehension. Not fully understanding the nature of my injuries, my brothers treated me gingerly. They each were far too cautious when playing around me. I reminded them constantly that I had a helmet on for protection, and I could still do most things that didn't require my getting hit or tackled hard. Though once in a while I tried to mix it up with them, I was considered "off limits" when it came to fighting. To her credit and my surprise, even Feenie managed to temper herself if I did something she didn't approve of.

After a week at home, I made my return to school. Mike Anthony, a pretty tough match for me even when healthy, laughed and called me "retarded helmet head" on my first day back. We had come to blows on two previous occasions, both ending in pretty much a draw.

He picked and picked on me all through science class. Mr. Hartley informed him his behavior was unacceptable, but he continued. He threatened to pull the helmet off "to show the class what Frankenstein looked like." When he slapped me in the helmet, Eddie told him he'd be talking to James right after class. He pushed Eddie hard to the floor, threatening to put him "in the same shape your retard brother is in."

I wasn't there to witness what happened during lunch that day, but Mike lost three teeth. Rumors abound. One had James informing Mike that payment for fucking with his sick brother was two teeth, while payment for fucking with his littlest brother was one tooth. It was said James even afforded Mike the choice of who would remove the teeth: James, Mike's dentist, or Mike himself. When Mike told him no one would be removing them, James felt he had no choice but to enforce his terms. The first punch knocked out Mike's upper two front teeth, while the second knocked out a bottom one on the left side.

Rumor also had it that James then stood amongst the crowd of onlookers and calmly proclaimed that those same terms applied to each and every person in the school who messed with me or Eddie. He made it clear those terms applied to first offenders only, saying "fuck with 'em once, I'll knock your teeth out. Fuck with 'em again, you won't get a third chance."

I'm glad Randy Weiss was a gentle giant. I can't imagine James being able to enforce those terms on him. Randy just went about his business, never going out of his way to create waves. But it was suspected amongst the student body that he could take anyone in the school, if he so desired, including James. Thank God it wasn't in his nature to see proclamations such as James' as any sort of challenge.

Needless to say, I didn't hear a single remark about how stupid I looked with my helmet for the duration of time in which I wore it. Even when kids pointed out how silly I looked in my hand-me-down oversized shoes, or with an embarrassing hole in a shirt or pair of pants, they later apologized, fearing I'd tell James. But they all refrained from remarking about the helmet, other than asking about how much longer I'd have to wear it.

The Old Man didn't say a single word to me for the entire post-accident first month. I wonder what was going through his mind. While he rarely said much to me or my brothers when he got home from work unless Feenie frenzied him into beating one or two of us, we could usually count on him for a little conversation on weekends. But even then, at least for the first month, he did not utter a single word in my direction.

On Saturday after my first week back in school, Jeff was talking to me about going hunting for Thanksgiving turkey, discussing the need to get one by Wednesday. During the conversation, I started to feel a little weird. I developed a sudden tunnel vision. I watched his mouth moving, but I couldn't understand what he was saying.

The next thing I remembered, I was being driven down the hollow in old man Webster's truck. An ambulance was waiting at the end of the hollow. By the time they strapped me to the gurney and put me in the ambulance, I was fully aware of everything occurring around me. I remained alert all the way to the hospital, responding quickly and clearly to all questions asked by the attending paramedic. I asked Feenie, who was riding in the ambulance with me, if I could go back home. The paramedic insisted we needed to see a doctor before I could go back home, saying he didn't hold the necessary authority to sign off on my release.

I spent yet another night in the hospital, though not being as thoroughly examined as I had been on my previous stay. When I got back home, Jeff walked off of the porch to greet me. He said "Mike, one minute you were staring out into space, the next you're on the floor, flopping around like a fish on land. Looked like something right out of the *Exorcist*."

He said Lee ran down to the Webster's to call the ambulance. Mr. Webster then apparently drove up to our house to get me and take me to the main road to meet the ambulance. Though I didn't recall much of what initially transpired, I did remember everything forward from the time I was driven those last fifty yards toward the waiting ambulance.

Feenie talked to my brothers about what to do if I had a seizure when she wasn't around. "It might look scary," she said. "It's best to just let it play out, unless you see him turning blue. That means he is having trouble breathing and may have swallowed his tongue, which means whoever is closest will have to reach into his mouth and pull it out of his throat."

I thought sarcastically "right. I can see any of my brothers jumping at the chance to reach into my slimy mouth to rescue me." I couldn't imagine doing the same for any of them. But, then again, perhaps if I really thought one of them might die if I didn't help, I'd probably close my eyes and do it.

I had four more seizures in the next few months. By the time the second one came, I began to notice symptoms, which allowed me to prepare. Tunnel vision was immediately preceded by a sudden queasiness. So as soon as I felt queasy, I simply lay down on the floor and let nature take its course. When the seizure was over, I asked any brothers close by if they had put their dirty hands into my mouth. Thankfully, on no occasion did I need rescuing.

I followed the same routine every morning. I'd put on my helmet, get pestered by Eddie until I took my medicine, then grab a peanut butter sandwich and head to school. On weekends and holidays, instead of school, I tossed mounds of dirt for Eddie to hit.

After about ten weeks, I finally got to take the helmet off. Eddie said I looked like Mike again. Feenie told me I had to take it easy for a few weeks. That wasn't a problem since it was mid January and already bitterly cold outside. Eddie and I went down to the creek anyway. We had to stay within earshot of the house, in case I had a seizure. The water was very cold, so we had to catch what we could from the creek bank using a fish net The Old Man brought home earlier in the year. Given the circumstances, it was a pretty good afternoon's catch, with each of us winding up with four.

My health gradually improved over the next few months. Spring was nearing and I was anxious to get back out in the creek. I had spent the whole winter being treated with kid gloves. It was unlike anything I had experienced before. Not physically fighting all the time was nice, but it came at far too steep a price. I wasn't allowed to play football or even wrestle with any of my brothers.

I steadily began to remember tiny bits and pieces about the day I fell. I remembered that I had been chasing Debbie Roe, a girl I had a crush on, before I slipped. I remembered veering out of the way, after rounding the corner, so I wouldn't run over two girls playing jacks on the sidewalk. I remembered sliding down the hill, thinking Mrs. Poston was going to punish me if she saw me all the way down at the railing. I remembered bracing for the impact with one the posts, all the while trying my very best to maneuver my body so I would hit it with something other than my groin area. I never did recall anything else before waking up in the hospital.

By mid-March, Lee started fighting with me again, saying "I'm gettin' sick of you getting off easy, while everyone else gets the shit beat out of them." I actually didn't mind fighting with him. I was happy he didn't feel the need to treat me so delicately. Unfortunately for him, James or Jeff usually came to my defense and roughed him up a bit each time he got the notion to fight.

I knew I was back to normal when Feenie and The Old Man started beating me again. Of course, at first, both were careful not to strike me about the head. However, after a while, Feenie didn't care where she hit, as long as she inflicted pain. Predictably, the beatings became more severe. Soon, it was just like old times. I was getting hit with ashtrays, pokers, cups, belts, etc...

In a peculiar way, I actually kind of welcomed it. While I detested the abuse, I was delighted they no longer saw me as a sickly child. I could finally play and do all the stuff my brothers did.

Springtime delivered warm temperatures. Eddie and I made our initial expedition up the creek earlier than usual that year. The water was cold, but provided we didn't stay in too long, we had a pretty fun time. We split our catch of twenty three crawdads evenly, with each taking eleven and placing the extra, smallest one back into the creek.

Chapter 9: The Car

By the time summer arrived, the fall from the top of the retaining wall was but a distant memory. I still had to take my medication daily, but I was doing everything my brothers did. I looked forward to a summer on the creek. Eddie worked a lot at the greenhouse, while James worked at the bakery. Donnie was getting big enough to help hoe the garden, and I was told to teach him how.

I was getting ready to head to the garden one morning, having just finished bringing in the day's water. I had just picked up the hoe when I noticed Mark Webster running up the hollow, toward our house. Though I couldn't make out what he was saying, there was undeniable urgency in his voice. The very moment he reached the yard, he looked straight at The Old Man and exclaimed "you have a call! Mom wants you to please come now!"

Knowing something extraordinary must had happened, Feenie, The Old Man and Mark Webster hopped into the brown Riviera and roared down the road. I still don't know how that big old car managed to get across the bridge that day. I could swear that, at no time racing across it, did all four tires touch the surface at the same time. The car swerved as it entered onto the bridge, with the front of the car pointed to the northeast. As it exited, it pointed to the southeast.

Rarely did anyone telephone The Old Man. Mr. Webster agreed to let my parents use his telephone in case of emergency. People would call their house and they, in turn, would send Mark up to tell us. I can recall only other such time they sent Mark up to tell The Old Man he had a phone call: the day when Old man Waybright got killed in a car accident.

As was always the case when Feenie and The Old Man were gone, Jeff was the de facto parent. Though I had little in common with him, Jeff was a good enough big brother. He teased us a bit, but he never beat us or asked us if we wanted to try his ice cream or anything like that.

He somehow knew what made each of my parents tick, and he used that understanding to position himself as confidant for each.

Four years older than I, he was much less excitable. He didn't seem to get beaten nearly as much as the rest of us. We couldn't be certain as to why, but James, Eddie, Lee and I wondered if he held a secret over Feenie she didn't want known. If he held one over her, then he likely held one over The Old Man, too, because even he seldom beat Jeff.

We liked Jeff because he fought so much with Joseph. Though they didn't live in the same house, when the two got together, they seemed to just end up fighting. If they spent twenty or fewer minutes together, a fight between the two could be avoided. However, as their time together increased, the probability of a fistfight increased at least as much. I don't know why they fought so much, but I was happy when Jeff got the better of it, like the last time they fought.

Six of us were playing a competitive little game of three on three. Jeff, The Old

85

Man and I teamed up against Lee, James and Eddie. Joseph was unable to control his emotions of not being selected to play in that particular game. He ran across the court and took the basketball, threatening to put a hole in it if he couldn't play. Though we all told him he'd get in the next game, he refused to give us back the ball.

Jeff told Joseph it was high time for him to stop acting "like a little Barbie doll."

Joseph made a few gestures at Jeff, motioning for him to go over and "just try to take the ball. I dare ya!"

Since both seemed equally willing, The Old Man told them to keep it clean. I guess he figured both would vent their respective differences and then we could get back to our game.

Before we even got into a good viewing position, Joseph tried to blindside Jeff. Knowing full well he might try something like that, Jeff bobbed his head back six inches, then immediately connected with a bone-crunching, straight left to Joseph's jaw, sending him straight to the ground. That was the first time I had personally witnessed a knockout.

Less than five seconds had passed before the time Joseph put the ball down to fight and the time he himself was on the ground. Though I was happy Jeff put him down quickly, I was a bit disappointed Joseph didn't take more of a beating that day.

While I hoped it not to be the case, I sensed that would be the last time they would fight, since it was so one-sided. I despised Joseph since the day he asked me to try his ice cream. I'm not sure why Eddie hated him. Maybe it was just because I hated him. I know we both cheered mightily for Jeff.

I asked Jeff why my parents left in such a hurry. He said "Eddie got hit by a car. He's in the hospital. Mom and Dad are headin' over there now."

Again, I refer back to those television shows. I had seen many where someone got hit by a car, only to end up laying in the middle of the road, either paralyzed and unable to move, or outright dead. Just a week earlier, I saw part a police show over at Granny's, where someone went through the windshield of a police car, leaving blood everywhere.

Fearing the worst, I anxiously asked Jeff "is he alive? Is he going to be able to come home?"

Of course he didn't know, but I think he sensed my concern, saying "he'll be ok, but he'll need to stay in the hospital for a while. He probably won't be home for a few days."

Though Jeff had always known I loved crawdad hunting, he never came down to the creek with Eddie and me. So when he said "come on, let's head down to the creek and catch some crawdads," I figured he was trying to help ease my mind.

Jeff and I spent the next couple of hours on the creek. He was never very good at catching crawdads. You've heard that saying "practice makes perfect?" Well, since he never practiced, I reasoned, I shouldn't have expected him to be very good. But I was fine with him just picking up the rocks and letting me do the catching. I was thankful he took the time and made the effort to get in the creek.

It was late when Feenie and The Old Man got home. I tried to wait up to see if Eddie was coming home with them, but I fell asleep on the floor in the living room next to Lee before they made it home. I don't know how I could have slept through the whole night, but it was morning when I woke up.

As soon as my eyes opened, I looked around for Eddie. He wasn't in the house. I really wanted to see him. I wanted to wake Feenie and The Old Man up to ask them how Eddie was. But I didn't dare touch that wool blanket. I knew if I woke them up, they would not let me ever go and see Eddie. I went down to the creek for a bit.

An hour passed, and I headed back home to make a peanut butter sandwich. The Old Man woke up, needing to pee. I followed him up to the outhouse and asked "is Eddie going to be ok?"

His eyes still focused on the outhouse door, he said "yep, but he's going to be in the hospital for a little while. He got pretty messed up."

"Can he walk?" I asked, hoping the news wasn't too bad. In some of those television shows, people couldn't walk again after they got hit by a car.

"Not yet, but he should be able to get up and around in a few days."

Relieved to hear that, I asked if we could go and see him. He said "not today or tomorrow. I'll take you over on Tuesday."

I was anxious for Tuesday to arrive. I was bored because I had no one to play with, so I went to the creek to try and pass the time. I was actually happy Tink and Sis came out to tease me. I could never throw a rock far enough to make it to their front porch, but Lord knows I tried. With each throw, they laughed and teased me about my "sissy" arm. I wished I could hit one of them squarely between the eyes with a sharp, pointy rock, but it was probably for the best that I didn't. Tink was a lot bigger than me. She probably would have beaten me up.

I woke up early on Tuesday. The sun hadn't become visible yet, but it started to get light outside. In the early morning, when we went outside to get the water, we'd see tons of worms just lying around on the ground. I figured they came up to bathe in the dew that drenched the early morning grass. Eddie figured they simply came out to drink. Regardless, to pass time, I set out to collect the ten biggest I could find.

As I walked down the steps, I was stunned by how many birds there were, walking about the yard, feasting. They all got their fill and left, and still there were lots of worms that hadn't made it back to their holes. It was on that Tuesday morning I finally understood that saying "the early bird gets the worm"

I collected ten or so of the largest ones before going back inside. Since it was still very early, I figured it best that I not try and wake my parents up, at least not directly. Though I dared not move the blanket, I managed to let them know I was ready to go to visit my brother. I jumped down off of the couch, onto the floor, over and over again. I knew I risked getting my butt whipped, but that was one whipping I would just have to take. I was going to see Eddie!

The Old Man peeked his head out from behind the blanket and shouted "what the hell is your problem? Can't you see we're trying to catch up on some sleep? Jesus, boy, I got half a mind to kick the livin' dog shit out of you." His tone was angry, but not serious enough to indicate that he'd throw on some pants and try to chase me down.

I stopped jumping, having achieved my goal. I had already got all the water needed for the day. It took me ten trips to the well, but I filled three five gallon buckets. Lee had enough to do the dishes and still have plenty left over for cooking, if he got a hankering to make some oatmeal.

I told The Old Man I already got the water and asked if we could go see Eddie. I was disappointed to learn visiting hours went from nine in the morning until eleven, then again from six at night until eight.

"Wake me up in about an hour. We'll get over there as soon as they open up visiting hours," he said.

Donnie came with us, asking my parents a lot of questions I already knew the answers to. My mind wandered, wondering what condition Eddie would be in. I imagined him in a whole body cast. I also imagined he'd have to wear a helmet, just like I did, after my fall.

The inside of the hospital seemed bigger than I remembered. Scores of immobile, old people sat in the front lobby. I figured some of them must have lived there, since they didn't appear to be going anywhere. Something was always being said over the intercom.

The Old Man grabbed me by the arm, knelt to one knee, and said "boy, when you see your brother, you don't touch him. They got him wrapped up pretty good, and he don't need you poking at him. If you touch him, you're only going to make him hurt more. You understand?"

I said I understood. I just wanted to see Eddie. I wanted to ask him when he could come home and catch crawdads.

Two beds filled the room. Nobody was in the one next to the doorway. Eddie was in the one next to the window, about fifteen feet from the door. His torso was all wrapped up, and he had casts on both his right arm and his left leg. His face looked ok, except for a large spot on his forehead wrapped in gauze. We used that same type of gauze many times over the course of our childhoods.

"Eddie!" I screeched, running toward him.

The Old Man grabbed me by the shirt and lifted me off the floor, saying "boy, what did I say? Don't touch him. You can talk to him, but you better not be poking at him."

Eddie's face lit up with a big smile. I reached down into my pocket and pulled out a night crawler, along with a handful of dirt I had managed to hide from Feenie and The Old Man until just the right moment.

Eddie and I always put a little bit of dirt in with the worms when we caught them, just to make them feel at home.

He couldn't move his arm well enough to take the worm from me, but I could tell he was happy with the gift. I sat the worm, along with the dirt, on a table next to the bed. Feenie wouldn't let him keep it, declaring "you can't bring this stuff into a hospital. There are lots of germs and you can make a lot of people in here even sicker than they already are."

"When are you comin' home, Eddie?" I asked. "I got two empty buckets. The creek is fillin' up with crawdads."

He didn't say too much at first. I think it must have hurt to start talking. After he started talking, he could easily finish what he was saying. But he seemed to have some problem when he started to say something. Making some pretty awful faces, he said "soon as the let me out."

I poked at the cast on his arm, asking "does that hurt?"

He replied "no. I can't feel any pain there, or on my leg. They itch a lot sometimes, especially at night. Now I know how James feels when he takes that wire brush to his arms," referring to how James used to scrub his arms completely raw, especially in the summertime, when sweat would aggravate his eczema. He'd sometimes scratch until we could actually see the muscles under his skin.

We went to the hospital each of the next four days. Each day, Eddie found it a bit easier to talk. By Thursday, he was able to use his core muscles to lift his head and back off the bed. By Friday, though he still looked badly beaten and bruised, he was talking and laughing, showing little of the pain and accompanying facial contortions I saw earlier in the week. I didn't go on Saturday, because The Old Man worked a double shift at General Tire.

Finally, on Sunday, The Old Man brought him home. Wearing crutches, he couldn't move very fast. I ran out the front door to greet him. His formerly dark blue and purple bruises were beginning to soften to yellow, some almost disappearing completely. I wanted to go crawdad hunting, but Feenie and The Old Man said there would be none of it until he got his casts off.

Those four weeks were rough. When he came to the creek with me, he had to sit on the bridge, while I caught the crawdads by myself. I often thought about trying to coax him into the creek, but I always stopped short. Not only would Feenie and The Old Man beat me senseless, I knew there was a good chance areas under casts could become infected with parasites from the creek water. For the same reasons we didn't drink it, I didn't want it getting into any of his open sores. Besides, an infection would only have meant more time for him not to be allowed in the creek, which would have defeated the whole purpose.

Sometimes, when Sis saw him sitting on the bridge, she would come out to talk to him. He tried act like he was as interested in crawdad hunting as he was in her, but he had a tough time balancing both. How could he be concentrating on crawdads if he was laughing with her, up on the bridge?

You know, looking back, I think he even liked her. Every time I talked bad about her, he would say something like "she's pretty funny," or "she's the only person I know who doesn't look down on us just because were poor."

Come to think of it, she never did make fun of me for being poor. Of all the things she teased me about, and there were many, including my sissy arm, my poor aim, my inability to catch every crawdad, and my funny haircut, she never once teased me about being poor. As I lie here, I grudgingly acknowledge she and her sister may not have been the spawn of the devil I once thought they were.

Even after Eddie finally had the casts removed, he had to wear a back brace for another month or so. Though he still couldn't bend well, or lift heavy rocks, he was allowed to get back in the creek. I was happy to see him getting back to normal. I think Granny felt sorry for him, because she didn't have him working for her the whole rest of the summer. He spent every morning in the garden with me, lightly hoeing and weeding. We spent almost every other waking hour that whole month on the creek.

September rolled around. It was a pretty uneventful month, other than suffering the annual anxiety of canning season and returning to school. October, however, produced the event that forever changed the family.

Chapter 10: The Well

I don't remember the exact date, but I know it was Saturday, because it was laundry day. I had already made countless trips to the well to bring in water on that miserable October morning. And I had to do it all alone, since Eddie was working at the greenhouse.

Cold drizzle had fallen for most of the day. Earlier, when I went out to get the first of the day's water, I wondered if I would see snow before the day was complete. Rain wasn't heavy that time of year, but once it started, it never seemed to stop. Weather followed the same pattern, year after year. Two weeks of light rain changed into a few weeks of cold drizzle. Drizzle turned into flurries. Soon, snow blanketed the ground for the rest of the winter.

Sunshine came in limited supply from October to April, breaking through the clouds once every three weeks or so. Eddie said he was going to move to one of those places he saw on the television where they played football in the sunshine in January. Places like Arizona or California or Hawaii.

Don't get me wrong, things weren't all bad in late fall and early winter. We looked forward to months of delicious venison. The garden didn't have to be hoed until the following April. Wet snow allowed us countless snowball fights. But the cold drizzle also meant we would soon be waking up cold, walking through that hollow, and freezing our butts off. It meant months of numb feet, numb ears and lots of fighting.

Lee washed clothes all day, and I brought bucket after bucket of water in from the well. We had been following a routine. I brought water in and he helped place it on the stove. In return, I helped him scrub clothes on the washboard until the water warmed on the stove. We both carried the old dirty laundry water out. Together, we filled the tub with clean water, then he started washing as I brought more water in.

I brought in what I believed to be the last four buckets needed. I helped Lee wash the remaining clothes in the tub and helped him hang them up on one of the three makeshift clotheslines we put up in the living room earlier. On gloomy days, we usually dried the clothes inside, to make sure we'd have clothes available for school on Monday. We'd usually get two sets washed and dried before The Old Man got home from the General Tire.

After Lee and I dumped the final tub of soapy water, we filled it up with fresh, warm water from top of the kitchen stove. I took off my shirt and kicked off my shoes, enjoying the warmth radiating from the coal stove.

Feenie popped her head out from behind the dark green wool blanket. "What the hell are you doing? You still have all of your dad's work clothes to wash. You'd better get off your ass and get some more water in here."

My heart sank. I thought "The Old Man's work clothes? That will mean three more tubs of water: one to wash his filthy shirts, one to rinse those shirts and wash his dirty pants and smelly socks, and one more to rinse those."

I complained "we've been washing all day and it is freezing outside. Can't we do that tomorrow?"

She replied "Ok. I see. You don't feel like getting a little cold and wet, huh?"

I guess I hadn't mastered the nuances of sarcasm yet. I was happy she saw things my way.

She slipped her shoes on and went out the back door. I figured she was going out to see for herself how nasty it was. "When she feels how cold it is out there, she'll understand," I thought.

She walked back into the house with a set of shackles The Old Man brought home a couple of months earlier to take over to the iron and metal junkyard to sell. I remembered playing cops and robbers with Eddie, locking them and unlocking them. We tried to run with them locked around our ankles.

She grabbed me by my right arm and dragged through the house, out to the well, where she routed one shackle behind one of the five legs that secured the well cover to the ground. She yelled at me to stand still as she clasped a shackle to my left leg, then my right. She abruptly turned and walked back into the house, ignoring my pleas to give me another chance.

Though the drizzle had let up a bit, transforming into a fine mist, each droplet that formed on my skin felt like ice. Two hours separated daylight from approaching darkness, when it would become unbearably cold. I tried to escape the shackles, but they were too strong. My only saving grace was that it was Bingo night. She'd have to let me out before she left for Bingo.

Using every ounce of energy I could muster, I tried again to break the chain attached to the cuffs. Needless to say, I failed miserably. I looked around for something to cut them off with. Any tool that might have stood a chance against them was fifty feet away, resting comfortably on the back porch.

I started to shiver. I saw Lee looking at me through the kitchen window, tears streaming down his cheeks. I didn't know if he was crying for me, or if Feenie had done something to him, like burned him with hot water, or hit him with a skillet. Either way, I knew he couldn't help. If it was James, I would have stood a chance of getting free. But Lee couldn't stand up to her.

I considered the worst. "I will freeze to death and become a statue forever," I thought. I hoped she would at least put me on the front porch once I was frozen. I didn't know if statues were capable of seeing, but if they could, I wanted to be on the front porch so I could see my brothers coming and going, even if I would never talk to them.

I then thought about how long it might be until The Old Man got home. "Although he didn't usually get involved in matters like this, he wouldn't allow her to let me just stay out here and freeze to death," I thought.

I did consider that she would try to convince him I did something so terrible that the only reasonable punishment was to chain me to the well. But even The Old Man would agree she overreacted, given the weather.

I huddled up next to the well. It felt colder than the surrounding air, so I was careful not to lean on it. I positioned myself to allow the well to help block any breezes. Even slight gusts felt like a million needles piercing my skin. Thank God the air wasn't blowing too hard.

My spirits lifted when I saw Eddie running towards the house. Granny had let him off early enough that he'd be able to make it home before dark. He just made it over the little wood bridge when I waved my arms, hoping to catch his attention.

He sprinted over to me. Seeing that I couldn't stop shivering, he ran into the house through the back door. As my eyes followed him, I saw Lee, still watching me, through the kitchen window. While demonstrating to him that I was getting very cold, Eddie ran out to me with a shirt and a big wool blanket. I didn't care the shirt was too small. I quickly put it on, then wrapped the blanket around me. I immediately felt much better, much warmer.

He asked "why did she put out here?"

"She got mad that I didn't want to bring more water in."

He said he was going to go inside and act like he was just getting home. He said he was going to try to find the key and open the shackles.

After a while, I heard him plead with Feenie to let me go. I heard him say he was going to get the police. Then I heard a bone-rattling slap, followed by Eddie's crying. Even after that, he pleaded with her to let me go.

I knew she had the final word, at least until James got home. "Feenie might beat James, but he would find a way to get the keys," I thought. James had been becoming more and more hostile toward her. A few days earlier, James told The Old Man he was ready for Feenie, declaring "if that bitch lays another hand on me, I'm gonna kill her. How she dies, I'll leave to you, Geezer."

About a week earlier, after she smacked Lee in the head with a skillet, James went so far as to tell The Old Man he'd prefer to strangle the very life out of her, so he could watch the look on her face as she slipped away. When he said "I'll cut her throat and make it quick, if you prefer," The Old Man slapped him across the face.

I think The Old Man knew if he wasn't home to stop it, James would eventually take her down, even if it meant getting stomped by The Old Man for doing it.

Eddie snuck me out a peanut butter sandwich and some cabbage. Sadness filled his eyes as he handed it to me. He said he wished it was him chained to the well, instead of me. A big, red handprint covered the left side of his face. Blood dripped out of the corner of his mouth.

"Mike," he said "I wish I could leave here. Other people don't live like this. When I collect money from the paper route, people let me inside their houses and....it's different...people just live different than us. I want to live in one of those places. I see kids in those houses with their moms and dads. They're not yellin' or beatin' each other, or talkin' 'bout killing each other. It ain't normal for kids to be thinkin' of ways to torture and kill their moms."

I really couldn't grasp what he was talking about. I assumed all parents treated their children as ours treated us. But since he began delivering papers the previous September, a job Feenie got him, he talked a lot about how other people lived. I was just happy it wasn't me who had to get up and walk that route in the winter with the weight of ninety newspapers.

"You need anything?" he asked. "I couldn't find the key. I think she has it in her bathrobe pocket."

"No. Just stay out here and talk to me. The Old Man will make her let me out of here as soon as he gets home."

He said "no, The Old Man is unloading a rail car at the foundry today. He probably won't be home 'til real late. I don't think she is goin' to Bingo, either. Otherwise, Jeff would be here to watch us."

I figured I was finished. She wouldn't let me out, no matter how much I cried and begged.

Eddie said "Mike, I gotta go find James. Soon as Feenie sees you covered up, she's going to put me here, and then we're both screwed. James will make her get you out of here. I promise I'll find him. I think he's playing pool at Hedrick's. I'll run there and I'll be back shortly."

Thinking about being tied up out there until The Old Man finished unloading a rail car was unpleasant. I didn't know what to say. While I knew it would mean being tied up for several more hours, I still didn't want Eddie to leave.

I finished the peanut butter sandwich, then went to the back side of the well, trying my best to hide the blanket from her view. "Please hurry, Eddie," I thought as I watched him run back down the hollow. But I knew that as long as I stayed wrapped in the blanket, I would not freeze to death, so long as it didn't start raining.

After about forty-five minutes, I saw Eddie and James running towards the house. Eddie was running as hard as he could to keep up. Darkness began to set in. James was screaming as he was running. I was sure Feenie could hear him, too, yelling "say your prayers, woman! You die tonight!"

My suspicions were correct. She met him at the door, a Pall Mall in her right hand and a big, glass ashtray in her left one.

He yelled at her "where's Mike?" He already knew the answer to that, because Eddie told him she had me chained up to the well.

She screamed back at him "none of your damned business. Get your ass inside! You and Eddie better have this place clean in half an hour!"

He stood resolute, undeterred by her screaming, and unwavering in his demand for the key. He never before physically fought with her, fearing The Old Man. But from the tone and anger of his voice, I felt that would soon change. He screamed at her "you got two minutes to get him away from that well!"

She yelled back at him "you don't tell me what I have!"

She then smacked James in the forehead with the heavy glass ashtray she was holding in her left hand, opening a huge gash that ran vertically from his

100

hairline to the bridge of his nose. Blood poured down his face, dripping off the tip of his nose.

She screamed again "I said get your ass inside and get this place clean. And I better not find a single drop of blood anywhere!"

I didn't see what happened immediately after that. James was inside. Eddie stood just outside the door, staring at the happenings inside with a concerned look on his face. I heard a lot of yelling and screaming, some gurgling, name calling, and slapping. Feenie and James each were doing their share.

I heard James yell "I said give me the key, you stupid bitch! Where is it?"

Then I heard Feenie, muffled, as if she was having some trouble breathing, say "here, take the fucking key. Take that little bastard with you and get the hell out of here."

James yelled a bit louder. "I ain't goin' anywhere, 'cept to let Mike out, then I'm comin' back and I'm gonna finish you off. This shit ain't happening no more. The Old Man won't stand up to you. I will. You are done. I'm puttin' an end to your shit, once and for all."

A tranquil, eerie silence fell over the house as James and Eddie came to unlock me. "What happened?" I asked.

"Don't worry 'bout it," said James. "Bitch ain't gonna pull any more shit like this. Old man is too big a pussy to do anything. He had his chances. This is bullshit. I'm going to go cut her damned throat."

As the three of us walked back into the house, Eddie pleaded with James not to kill her. Not because he had any special feeling for her, but he didn't want to see James get killed by The Old Man.

We stepped inside the house. Expecting a big fight-to-the-death, I braced myself. Strangely, it was quiet. "Wait," I thought. "Was that crying I heard coming from Feenie's room?" Yes, it was. I don't ever recall hearing her cry before. I thought maybe James hurt her pretty badly.

She hadn't made him cry one time with her beatings since he was eight. Some four years later, the tables had turned. James had established a new order. The Old Man was still the man of the house, but there was no doubt Feenie would have to deal with James much differently than she ever had before.

I usually never so much as even touched the blanket covering her doorway. But I had to know what was going on. I poked the blanket. No yelling or screaming pierced the air. I poked it again. Still no response. I reached for the blanket, frightened that Feenie would pummel me as soon as she noticed me. I peeled it back just enough that I could peek with just one eye.

She had her back to me. She was filling up a garbage bag with her clothes. I didn't understand. "Why her clothes? Why not James'? Surely she'd have The Old Man take him and dump him on the side of the road," I thought.

But she just kept taking her clothes out of the dresser and filling up the garbage bags.

James was at the sink, washing his forehead. After a couple of minutes, he picked up a tube sock from the floor and pressed it against the gash. A few minutes passed, and though he remained prepared for battle, he was no longer thinking of slitting her throat. He sat on the couch with a poker in his hand. If she came out of her room wanting more, he would have been more than happy to oblige.

After about six or seven minutes of uncomfortable silence, she came through the blanket with two garbage bags full. A huge knot protruded from her forehead and a sizeable cut ran across her left eye. James had punched her at least twice to get the key to set me free. I guess most any kid would feel distressed seeing his mom like that. But I didn't. I felt nothing, indifferent.

As she walked out of the house, James stared at her. She looked at me, as if she wanted to say something, but didn't. At that moment and for the first time in my life, I had seen my mother vulnerable. At that moment, at least to me, she was not Feenie. She was Mom.

She did not look back at James. She didn't want to buy any more of what he was selling.

As she walked down those steps toward that old sixty-three Chrysler, I glanced over at Eddie. He had disbelief in his eyes. I think he was relieved James had calmed down. But I think he was saddened the evening turned out like it did.

Feenie said nothing to any of us before she drove away.

From that day forward, things were very different. She left us for the first time that night. At first, we were happy. But after a while, we began to realize the effect it was having on The Old Man. He rarely came home before ten or so at night. He spent just enough time to get a little sleep, then left for work before the kids got up.

I wonder where she is right now. I've heard people say mothers somehow just know if any of their children are in trouble. I wonder if she even senses something bad has happened to me. If I don't make it out of here, I'll probably get a bird's eye view of her, provided she decides to come to my funeral. Even if I manage to somehow survive, I don't expect her to feel any guilt for what has happened to me. I don't envision her capable of that emotion.

Either way, I know she will never forget that night when she was knocked off of her throne.

Chapter 11: The Attic

The house on Knapp Street was an old, run-down, two story shack. Covered with crumbling, brown, tar shingles, it must have been once of the first houses built when the town was founded.

With almost no front yard to speak of, it certainly didn't hold the play value of the old shack. It stood in the middle of a row of old houses, with two houses on each side. It seemed more a part of a senior community than a single family home. Old people lived in each of the surrounding houses.

Moving into town from the hollow was a condition Feenie placed on The Old Man in exchange for her permanent return. She told him she did not want to live so far from town, in case there was an emergency. I think fear of James had more to do with it. Either way, The Old Man agreed, and they moved us away from the only home I had ever known.

James and Feenie formed a "don't-mess-with-me-and-I-won't-mess-with-you" relationship. They hardly ever spoke to each other, and they never again came to physical confrontation. Even when he wasn't working, James was hardly ever home, preferring to shoot pool over at Hedrick's. Feenie and The Old Man didn't set a time for him to be home. They agreed that as long as he went to school, they would not ask anything else of him.

I didn't like the house much. We spent too much time inside. Feenie hardly ever let us go outside to play, saying she didn't want us destroying the neighborhood. If we promised to go to the junior high school to run around, we could occasionally pry an "ok" out of her.

Inside, we had to remain quiet, careful to not disturb her. While television held tremendous appeal at first, it quickly lost its novelty. Before we had a television, I thought people who had them were lucky. After spending so many nice days parked in front of one, I began to feel quite the opposite.

I don't think Feenie liked the house very much, either. She seemed to take on the general feeling of the house. Studying the house from the outside, one would think its many windows allowed for plenty of natural light to brighten it. However, most of the interior rooms were so dark we needed to have lights turned on in the daytime, just so we could see well enough to get around.

She spent a lot of time in her bedroom. In fact, I didn't see much of her at all the whole time we lived there. She came out in the morning to grab coffee, then went straight back to her room. She came downstairs in the afternoon for about an hour before she headed off to Bingo, giving each of us a list of chores she wanted completed before she returned. She usually didn't make it back until after all the kids were asleep.

School was due to start in about a week. I was going into the fourth grade. When we lived in the old shack, the beginning of the school year meant an end to summer fun spent exploring and hunting crawdads. But things were different in the new place. I actually looked forward to going back to school. I'd rather have been at school, where I could at least play during recess and talk with other kids, than be confined to the inside of that dark, quiet house.

Eddie always got excited that time of year, regardless of where we lived. Rather than focus on what he'd be giving up, he preferred to focus on the benefits of school. Though I hated the thought of returning in those hand-me-down clothes, he didn't seem to mind that all the other kids made fun of us for being so poor. He used to say "I'm gonna change that. Someday those kids will be working for me."

Feenie told us we were to stay inside. We tried our best to persuade her to allow us outside, but she quickly countered anything either of us had to offer. When she insisted we couldn't be trusted not to disturb the peace and quiet of the neighborhood, we promised we'd be quiet and look for worms. When she said she didn't want us tracking mud in and out of the house, we told her we would use garbage bags to kneel on while we dug. When she said we'd get sick from being out in the rain, we figured she wasn't going to let us go outside, no matter how hard we tried.

I didn't understand why she wanted to keep us inside. We would have been happy to head back over to the junior high to play football or anything, so long as it was outside. Plus, if we were outside, there was no chance of us getting on her nerves.

Nevertheless, we understood she was determined, so we made the best of it. After watching that television for some fifteen minutes, we decided to turn it off and play. We needed to find ways to run off excess energy, but Feenie hadn't yet returned to her room yet that morning. If she had been held up in her room on the second floor, we would have likely held one of our patented broad jumping contests in the living room on the first floor, pushing the smaller sofa an inch or two farther away from the larger sofa for each successive jump, until one of us didn't quite make a legal, Olympic-sanctioned jump.

Earlier, she had been sitting at the kitchen table thumbing through the newspaper, looking for food bargains. We hadn't heard her clomping back up the stairs, so we figured we had a few minutes to chase each other before calm was to be forced on us. We ran up and down the stairs, chasing each other with garter snakes we caught near a ditch, down around the junior high, a day earlier. I ran after him, chasing him through the living room. He slipped when rounding the corner to the kitchen and stumbled into the back of Feenie's legs.

She immediately turned around and threw her coffee on him. He hadn't even started screaming from the hot coffee before she grabbed him. With his right forearm firmly in her left hand's grasp, she took her free hand and smacked him in the head about six or seven times with a box of oatmeal, the object nearest her hand at the time. Had we known it was one of those very rare mornings when she cooked, we would have been more careful. We probably wouldn't have even gone near the kitchen.

After she finished beating him, she violently jerked him by the arm, making her way toward me. She reached for a handful of hair, but it hadn't grown long enough for her to grab anything meaningful. Perhaps she could have pinched a little between her index finger and thumb, but she clearly couldn't grab enough to do any damage. I think she forgot for a moment that she had given us our monthly buzz cuts just ten days earlier. Frustrated, she wrapped her right hand around my left ear.

She marched us both up to the attic, twisting Eddie's forearm and my ear to the point we were more than willing participants in the march. She pushed Eddie in hard, causing him to bounce off a beam that went from the floor to the ceiling. He screeched, grabbing his shoulder. She pushed me in just hard enough that I crashed into Eddie, causing us both to fall to the floor. Before slamming the door shut, she said

"I'll be back later to collect your bodies and bury you after the rats and spiders get through with you."

She remained just outside the door for several seconds, lingering as she always did, hoping to hear one of us say something bad enough to justify a beating. Hearing nothing she deemed "beating worthy," she left after thirty seconds or so, muttering something about how she couldn't believe her life turned out like it did.

I secretly wished she had lingered a bit longer, at least until our eyes had adjusted a bit to the sudden blackness. I don't remember ever being utterly frightened like I was in that moment. Eddie and I literally couldn't even see our hands in front of our faces. We managed to locate each other by sound. We huddled near the beam Eddie was so brutally slammed into just a short time earlier.

"Eddie, I hate rats," I said, trembling, figuring they were already flanking us, preparing to launch an attack. It's amazing what darkness can do to the mind. I could see twenty rats in daylight in various states of attack preparedness, and I could quickly figure out twenty different ways to take them down. But in the darkness, I couldn't tell what those vermin were up to. "I can handle the spiders, but can you take care of the rats?"

Eddie quickly responded "yep, I'll take care of the rats. You just let me know where you think one is, and I'll try to scare it off."

We quickly grew silent, figuring that if they were coming for us, we might hear them, giving us a chance to launch an effective counter attack.

While we knew they had the sight advantage, we still had size. And contrary to any reports you may hear otherwise, size *does* matter. We reckoned that they'd probably get in their share of good bites and scratches, but we were going to take a lot of them down with us.

We figured that if we heard them far enough in advance, we might even give them pause by stomping on a few before they could inflict any real damage. We

108

reasoned that any military, including one made up entirely of rats and spiders, might think twice about attacking, if we simply showed them the costs of doing so would be too high.

Several minutes of complete silence were suddenly interrupted with Eddie's giggling. "What did she hit me with, anyway?" he asked.

I whispered "it was the oatmeal box. And you're lucky. The rolling pin was only a couple of feet away. If she'd gotten her hands on that, you'd be in a world of hurt."

"Yeah, you're probably right," he whispered back, "but that didn't hurt one bit. The coffee burned, but the oatmeal box? If she thinks that hurt, she needs to find better weapons."

We called her names and giggled a bit more. And though it was still very dark, my eyes had adjusted a bit. I was at least able to make out a general outline of Eddie.

Feenie must have heard us. She marched up the stairs, her legs forcefully stomping the old wood floor, announcing her fury in advance. She launched the door open and came in swinging a belt. She caught Eddie three or four times and got me three good times. As she stomped out, she screamed that we wouldn't be getting any lunch.

While that was an inconvenience, I was much more concerned about all the rats and spiders scheming to kill and eat us. The moment she flung the door open, I glanced around the attic, hoping to gather enough intelligence to prepare a strong defense. But they never showed themselves. They must have scurried when they heard her stomping up the stairs. I was a bit distressed that none gave away their positions. Clever little creatures!

I thought about how things would have unfolded if we still lived in the old shack. Since there was no attic, she would have beaten us a bit and just tossed us outside, where we could always find apples or wild grapes or berries to eat. In emergencies, we had the garden from which we could steal a tomato or two.

In the new house, no lunch meant exactly that – no lunch. Fortunately, we were smart enough to know to eat a lot when we first woke up, if we could find anything. Peanut butter and bread could usually be found, so we would gorge on sandwiches before she made her way downstairs.

We had been huddled, sitting back to back for about thirty minutes, when suddenly we began to hear noises from near the west wall. Obviously, something other than the old books and wood that generally occupied that area was over there. My heart began racing, certain the rats had retreated when Feenie made her second trip up, formed a different plan, and were amassing to launch an all out attack. "I think they're getting ready, Eddie," I whispered, suddenly feeling the urge to go to the bathroom.

Eddie didn't seem to be as alarmed as I. He said "we're a lot bigger than rats. We probably look like Godzilla to them. They wouldn't take the chance of attacking us first, unless they're crazy rats. Besides, the plan is no different now than it was before. We'll hear them coming, stomp on a few, and chances are they'll leave us alone for good." I hoped that to be the case, but I had a tough time calming down for the next couple of hours.

Though still very dark up there, our eyes had again adjusted a bit, aided by a tiny sliver of natural light shining through under the door. Knowing we would be able to see a little bit, at least until nightfall, helped to ease the terror slightly. We hoped to be let out before nightfall. Otherwise, it would become very dark, meaning we would have to fend off the rats and spiders in pitch black.

Sometime in the middle of the afternoon, the attic door began to slowly open. I figured Feenie was coming in to beat us some more because she hadn't yet heard us screaming in terror. Strangely though, we hadn't heard her stomping up the stairs to announce her arrival.

To our relief, it was Lee.

"Eddie, c'mere," he said in a hurried and hushed tone. "I brought you and Mike a sandwich and some water. I could only bring one sandwich and one glass, so you'll have to share. If Mom saw me with two of each, then she'd know that I was making 'em for you two."

We said we understood, and thanked him. We weren't real hungry, but we didn't know how long we were going to be there, so we knew we should eat and drink.

As Lee was leaving, I asked "Lee, can you turn the hall light on? It's pretty dark in here, but we can see a little bit with the light that's coming from under the door. Once night comes, we won't be able to see at all. The rats and spiders will have a big advantage."

Lee said he would, as he carefully closed the door, nervous that Feenie might be wondering where he was. If she didn't hear him about the house, cleaning or making her coffee, she would have assumed he was helping us and would have put him in there with us.

Eddie and I put our faces down to the floor and watched as he walked away. After a few seconds, a tiny bit of artificial light came shining through the crack under the door.

As night approached, we spent ten or fifteen minutes planning how to defend ourselves from the inevitable cowardly nighttime attack. We figured that since they hadn't attacked all day, they spent the entire time working together, scheming to take us down. To defend ourselves from the onslaught, we decided we would stand back-to-back and kick and stomp anything that came to get us. We also figured it best to fight them by swinging the denim shorts we were wearing.

We would have preferred to be wearing shoes. But we hadn't planned on the day turning out as it had. Neither of us had shoes on earlier when Eddie ran into Feenie, so we had to make do with the shorts. We pulled off our shorts and each held a pair by one leg. They felt heavy enough that we would be able to kill spiders and at least hurt the rats enough to make them think twice about attacking us.

Remaining ever vigilant for a surprise attack, Eddie and I began talking about the old house in Cravensdale. He talked about the Indian. I talked about crawdad hunting. We talked a little bit about Lee. We agreed that as bad as things were, poor Lee had the worst of it.

We stayed up in that attic the whole day and a good portion of the evening. When The Old Man got home and let us out, Feenie told him we intentionally tried to knock her down so she would burn herself with coffee. He whipped us with the belt, then told us to get a sandwich and get to bed.

Lee was in the room when we got there. He asked "you guys ok?"

We thanked him again for the water and the sandwich he gave us earlier. We knew he had made it for himself, but had given up his lunch for us. We told him we must have had a guardian angel up there. We spent the whole day in that attic ready to fight rats and spiders, but didn't end up having to.

I didn't know why they didn't attack us. Maybe they felt sorry for us. Maybe they liked listening to our stories. Or maybe they just weren't hungry enough to take the chance. Either way, I was pretty happy to be out.

Feenie went to Bingo soon after The Old Man got home. Eddie and I snuck out of the bedroom. We wound up playing outside in the mud for an hour or so in the dark, catching worms. We snuck back inside, took a bath, and were in bed, faking sleep, when Feenie got home. I figured she must have had a good night at Bingo. She didn't even come up to yell at us.

After two short months, we moved out of that house and into the one at Highland Park. I don't know why we left, but the house was demolished shortly after we left. The Old Man helped to tear it down.

Chapter 12: Cat Fight

From the outside, the Highland Park house seemed nice enough. Covered in green shingles on the outside, it certainly was the nicest looking house of the three I lived in. An enormous one hundred and twenty year old oak tree dominated the small front yard. A big garden lay directly behind the back yard, which ran thirty feet deep.

Although still too small for such a large family, the inside was nice. A nice, modern bathroom had a shower, a first in any home I lived in. It had two bedrooms, just like the old shack, but they were much nicer. The living room and kitchen were both larger than the shack. Carpeted throughout, I imagined a winter free of persistently numb feet.

I remembered Eddie talking about the carpet in people's houses when he collected for his paper route, but I never imagined it so easy on the feet. I also didn't imagine it would require so much work to keep clean.

While it looked pretty, some bizarre stuff happened in that house. I think it was haunted. For such a short time spent there, I sure have a lot of memories.

One night, James, Eddie, Lee and I were sleeping in the bedroom. We had only been in the house for three weeks or so. Donnie and Timmy were still pretty little. They slept on top of a blanket on the floor of The Old Man and Feenie's room. Jeff slept on the couch in the front room.

Earlier that night, Eddie and I caught some fireflies. The Old Man watched some Westerns, took a bath, and went to bed so he could get up early for work. Feenie came home from Bingo at about ten thirty. She wasn't in a bad mood. We all went to sleep shortly after she got home.

No air conditioning, combined with body heat generated from so many children closely packed together, made sleeping uncomfortable. After the sun went down, we opened many of the windows, placing blocks of wood under them to keep them propped up. When we got up in the morning, we simply removed the blocks and let the windows down. That approach allowed us to keep bees from overrunning the house. For some reason, we hardly ever saw bees in the house at night. We saw and killed many in the day, but very few at night. I figured they went to sleep a little earlier than kids did.

Sometime during the night, I woke up to pee. We didn't have to worry about drinking a lot of water in that house. If we needed to pee in the middle of the night, we just walked the twenty feet to the toilet.

As I made my way back into the room, I saw something out of the corner of my eye. It scampered under the bunk bed. James and Lee were sleeping on the floor. I figured whatever it was must have been getting ready to eat them and, not wanting to get caught in the act, ran under the bed when I came walking back to the room. It was fairly dark, but light from the moon allowed me to see well enough to get back and forth.

I whispered to James. "James... James....James!" I didn't want to go into the room to wake him up, believing whatever went under the bed would jump out and get me. I didn't know what to do.

Glancing around, I saw a bucket of toy soldiers just inside the door. I cautiously picked up the three or four of the soldiers and threw them at James, one at a time. The third one hit him in the face.

He woke up angry. "What the hell are you doing? Can't you see it's the middle of the night?"

I whispered to him "there's something under the bed."

James jumped to his feet. If there existed a list of things James fears, it wouldn't have much on it. But at the top of that list would be *the unknown*.

His voice changed from anger to concern. "What is it?"

"I don't know. I was coming back from the bathroom and I saw something run under the bed."

James remained inside the room. Eddie and Lee were still sleeping. Eddie was on the top bunk, so he wasn't in any immediate danger. Lee was on the floor.

"Lee, wake up!" James said, reaching down to shake him, keeping his eyes on the area under the bed.

Lee finally woke up and asked what was going on. James told him "Mike says there's something under the bed." Lee asked what it was and we told him we didn't know.

Never taking his eyes off of the bed, James whispered "Mike, go and get The Old Man. Lee and I will stay here and make sure it doesn't get Eddie."

I ran down to The Old Man's room and burst inside. As soon as the door opened, The Old Man shouted "godammit, this had better be important. I got to go to work in three fuckin' hours and I'm still tired. Why do you little bas..."

"Dad! Dad! Dad!" I interrupted. "There's somethin' under the bed. It's real big!"

I think he knew from the tone of my voice something out of the ordinary had happened. Believe me, we had learned over time if we were going to wake him, it had better be for a very good reason.

The Old Man sprang up out of bed and ran down to the room, stubbing one of his toes on a toy fire truck Donnie forgot to put away after playing with it earlier. James and Lee were still in the room, making sure whatever was under the bed didn't get Eddie.

The Old Man flipped on the light, asking "where is it?"

"Mike said it went under the bed," James told him.

The Old Man dropped to the floor and stared intently under the bed. After jumping back to his feet, he proclaimed "it's a damned bobcat." He then walked away, down the hall toward his bedroom.

I thought he was going back to bed. I wondered how we were going to get it out of the room. I never had to fight with a bobcat, but judging from what people said about them, I figured it probably was not smart to fight with it, if we could avoid it.

I was relieved to see The Old Man coming back down the hallway. He had put on pants and a shirt. I guess he had heard the same things about bobcats I had. His right hand held his thick leather work belt.

In all the commotion, Eddie woke up. He started to jump off of the top bunk. James screamed "stay there, Eddie!"

Eddie stopped in his tracks. Lee must have been looking under the bed, because Eddie was studying Lee's face. "What is it, Lee?" Eddie asked.

Lee told him "Dad says it's a bobcat."

Eddie quickly wrapped himself in the wool blanket he was previously sleeping on top of. He scooted himself away from the edge of the bed. He turned to James and asked "James, does he look like he's mad?"

James responded "yep, and he'll rake your damned face off, if you piss him off enough."

Eddie covered his face with the blanket, then curled up, his face firmly planted in the mattress.

The Old Man entered the room. "How the hell did it get in here?" he asked us.

"I don't know," I said. "He must have come through the window."

The Old Man pondered for few moments. He shouted to Jeff in the front room. "Jeff, get your ass up, now!"

Jeff muttered something from the front room. The Old Man shouted at him "check the back door. If it's shut, open it. And open the front door, too."

After Jeff opened the front door, The Old Man went toward the bed. James and Lee backed out of the room, toward the hallway. We crowded the doorway so we could see the action that was about to take place.

The Old Man reached over and ripped the mattress from the bottom bunk. The large brown and gray cat bore its teeth as he stared back up at The Old Man through the springs of the bottom bunk. Its evil hiss gave me goose bumps. "KWWOOOOOWWWLLLL!!!!!" Though not as loud as a lion, it was still louder and deeper than I expected.

The hiss only seemed to make The Old Man more determined. After all, it was The Old Man's house and nobody, man or animal, was to challenge him.

He grabbed the whole bunk bed with his left hand and pulled it from the wall. He swung the belt buckle at the cat. I think the cat must have been surprised his hissing and growling didn't scare The Old Man off. Every time he hissed, he got hit with the buckle.

Eddie was still on the top bunk. Every once in a while, he peeked his head out, but when he heard a hiss, he immediately covered himself back up. He later told me he was torn, wanting to see the action, but not wanting to be part of it.

The cat began looking for a way out. It tried to get out through the window. But sometime during the furor, the wood block that held the window up must have got knocked free, because the window was down. For all I know, the cat could have bumped it when he came in.

On the window sill and realizing it couldn't make it out, it jumped onto the top bunk. Eddie knew the cat was right next to him, so he curled up even tighter. The Old Man didn't want the cat up there so close to Eddie, so he swung the belt at him. The cat rose up on its hind legs and hissed again at The Old Man, seemingly waiting for the right opportunity to jump on The Old Man, so it could rake his face off.

Eddie couldn't take it any longer. He sprang from under the blanket, jumped off the bed, and ran right past us, not looking back to see if the cat was following him. He later said he figured that if he could make it to his brothers, we could all fight the cat together. He said he knew he alone couldn't beat the cat, nor did he want to try.

After Eddie made it through the door, he joined us at the doorway to watch the ongoing battle. Neither The Old Man nor the bobcat gave any ground. A classic "good versus evil" match, I was waiting for The Old Man to deal the blow that would finally send the cat on his way. The thought crossed my mind that maybe the cat didn't want to leave. "Perhaps it just decided to move in, and was challenging The Old Man for control of the house."

The Old Man whacked the cat hard on its side. The cat sat on its hind legs, hissed and, for the first time in the fight, swung back at The Old Man face. I think it missed its mark by less than inch.

I then witnessed something I never in my life thought I would see: *The Old Man began to slowly back out of the room!*

His eyes remained focused on the cat as he backed his way towards the door. Eddie, James, Lee, Jeff and I backed out into the hallway as he approached. Once at the door, he reached slowly to the knob and put his hand around it. As soon as he got a firm grip on the handle, he shut the door as fast as he could.

James looked up at The Old Man and said "little tougher than you thought, ain't he?"

The Old Man seemed agitated. He also seemed relieved to be out of the room. "I ain't finished yet. I'll give him a little while to calm down, then I'll get his ass out of there."

An idea struck him. "Lee and James, You two run around the back and open the window from the outside."

But James would have none of it, proclaiming "I ain't havin' no pissed off bobcat jumpin' out the window and killin' my ass before I can make it back inside."

The Old Man stared at James, ready to say something, but didn't. He took Jeff outside with him. They ran around the house and opened the bedroom window. After about fifteen seconds, they came running back into the house. The Old Man told Jeff to go shut the back door, while The Old Man shut the front door. He turned to the group of us still standing in the hallway, saying "it should go out on his own. We'll wait about five minutes. It'll be long gone by then, and you kids can get your asses back to sleep."

A few minutes went by. He told Jeff to open the bedroom door. Nervously, Jeff grabbed the knob and slowly turned it. He inched the door open, looking down at where a bobcat might be if it was ready to spring an attack. Nothing was there. He opened it about two more inches. Still nothing. He slowly pushed it open just a little more. He caught a glimpse of the cat, resting on the top bunk. He quickly shut the door, saying it looked like the cat had never moved.

The Old Man knew he had to draw up a plan. To that point in my life, I don't ever remember having to make up a *plan B*. The Old Man had always executed *plan A*, and there was never a need for a different plan.

I imagined he'd just get a gun and shoot it. He could have chosen any of his thirty-five gun collection to kill it. I figured the only reason he hadn't shot it earlier was because he didn't like the taste of bobcat. If it was a deer, it likely would have already been hanging upside down, getting skinned.

He made certain everyone completely understood the plan. He, Jeff, James, and Lee were to go into the room, each armed with a big wool blanket. If the cat jumped at one of them, that person was to throw the blanket over himself. The others would then throw blankets on the bobcat, tie him up and get him out of the house. Eddie and I were supposed to go to Feenie's room, where Donnie and Timmy were still sleeping.

They all four went into the room. Eddie and I stayed outside the door, listening for clues as to what was happening. They came out in just a few seconds. I asked James what happened. He said "The Old Man threw his blanket on top of it and it got out from underneath it and jumped out of the window."

The Old Man seemed pretty proud of himself, smiling as he proclaimed "no damned cat is going to take over this house. I'm the man of the house! If that damned cat wants to stay here, he'd better ask my permission next time. Plus, if he wants to stay here, he's gonna have to pay rent"

Never one to let an opportunity to needle The Old Man slip by, James looked at him and said what I was thinking. "That cat was man of the house while he was here. You're lucky he decided to leave."

"I'd have kicked his ass all over that room," said The Old Man. "I was just trying to get you boys out safely, which I did."

James had to agree with that, but told The Old Man he sure looked scared when the cat decided to take a swing.

The Old Man responded "look, I could've gone in with a baseball bat. By now you'd be cleaning up cat guts. Next time, I'll just mash its damned head and you can clean up the mess. Now I'm goin' back to bed. Keep that window closed for the rest of the night, unless you want him to come back. If he does, then you'll be the ones getting rid of him. I ain't got time to fight no damned bobcat."

We went back into the bedroom, reliving every second of the encounter. Jeff went back to the front room. He didn't let on like it was as big a deal as it was. Eddie, James, Lee, and I stayed up till daylight talking about the encounter. It ended up being one on the best nights ever.

Chapter 13: Horns and a Pitchfork

Nothing out of the ordinary happened in the eight days that passed since the bobcat got into the house. Things had begun to settle back to normal. Eddie was working at the greenhouse with Grandpa Joe and Granny. Lee was cleaning the house. It was Monday, the second of the two straight days during the week in which James didn't work at the bakery.

Earlier, James and Lee got into a fight, right in the middle of the kitchen. Lee resented that James didn't work around the house. James reasoned that since Feenie took all of his money he made from the bakery, he didn't have to work around the house. For her part, Feenie didn't ask him to also work at the house. While I'm certain she would have liked to have him do chores, I think she felt that was likely to start a fight she knew she couldn't win.

I'll give Lee this much: no matter how badly James beat him, he was always ready for another go. I asked him once why he always fought with James, knowing the likely outcome. He said "one of these days, he'll screw up and walk into one, and it's gonna hurt," explaining that eventually one of his flailing, windmill overhand rights would find its mark. "He'll probably still kick my ass, but I'm gonna enjoy watching him bleed."

Feenie sent James to the bedroom. He presented a difficult challenge for her. Since their big fight, she had given up on trying to discipline him by force or threat of force. If he got on her nerves, rather than yelling or screaming or doing anything that might provoke a fight, she sent him to the bedroom, leaving him for The Old Man to deal with. The Old Man beat James to try and get him to mind his mother, but it didn't work. I don't think any amount of beatings could make that a reality. Eventually, even The Old Man gave up on beating him.

Feenie took Jeff and the baby with to town, barking orders on her way out the front door. She shouted to Lee "those damned dishes had better be done, and the house had better be clean by the time I get back!" I was sitting on the top step, tying my hand-me-down generic work boots, when she loudly asked "why in the hell are you still here, when weeds are out there trying to take over the garden?" I immediately sprinted to the garden, hoe in hand.

I had been hoeing and weeding for thirty minutes or so before I went into the house to get some water. A half put together jigsaw puzzle sat on the coffee table. Unlike many of Feenie's puzzles, the pieces weren't too small. On top of that, I was drawn to the picture on the box of what the completed puzzle looked like, a red lighthouse overlooking a rugged beach and a calm, light blue ocean. I figured it wouldn't hurt to try and put some of it together.

I guess I had been working on the puzzle for about twenty minutes when, suddenly, a loud noise – much like a big gun going off – resonated throughout the house. I jumped to my feet, thinking maybe Lee had finally had enough, and shot James. I quickly determined that not to be the case when Lee ran to doorway of the kitchen, asking "what the heck was that?"

In less than the time I could respond with an "I don't know," James had sprinted down the hallway and was already headed for the door. "RUN!" he screamed as he sprinted past me. The speed of his movement and the tone of his voice let me know without doubt that something very frightening had just taken place.

My mind said "RUN," but my body couldn't comply. I can't explain it, other than I literally was so scared I couldn't move. I knew at that instant how Eddie must have felt when he first saw that Indian man on the creek out at the old house.

James made it out to the big oak tree in the yard. He was quickly joined by Lee, who, judging from how hard the back door hit the side of the house as he ran outside, understood the urgency in James' voice. I could see them both through the open front door, but I still couldn't run to them.

James saw me standing there in the middle of the living room, and motioned for me to get out of the house. Sensing that I wanted to run but somehow just couldn't, he sprinted back up toward the house, stopping about two feet from the doorway. Standing only ten feet or so away from me, he yelled out "Mike, c'mon, get out of the house!"

Though his voice lost none of its urgency, my body finally did what my brain told it to do. I raced as fast as I could out of the house, past the oak tree. James and I ran together about another hundred yards down the gravel road. Lee was well ahead of both me and James. Once we got to where we believed was a safe distance, we stopped, breathing heavily. I asked James what happened.

"The fuckin' devil, that's what happened!" he exclaimed.

I didn't know what the devil looked like, but I hoped and prayed that a towering red figure, replete with horns, tail and pitchfork, wasn't going to pop out of the front door and start chasing us.

I thought I'd have a better chance without the boots, so I slipped them off. Hey, given the choice of two torn up feet or being dragged to Hell to burn for eternity, which would you elect?

We decided to get a little further away from the house. We walked backwards, keeping an eye on the house, ready to turn and sprint should the devil start chasing us. Actually, I didn't keep my eyes on the house. I didn't want to see the devil. If James started running, I figured, I would just start running with him. Besides, I thought I remembered hearing a rule that I had to *see* the devil before he could take me to Hell with him, so it was to my advantage to keep my eyes pointed at the ground.

After we made it out of sight range of the front porch, we turned and began walking forward. We caught up with Lee, who had made it all the way to the North School, some five minutes later. James told Lee what he saw, and Lee agreed that none of us should go back into the house until we got the devil out.

I thought I remembered hearing that someone had to do something pretty bad to get the devil himself involved. "James, what did you do to piss the devil off?" I asked, thinking maybe he kicked a dog or a cat, or stole some money from Ms. Schmidt.

"I ain't done jack shit, at least nothing bad enough to get the damned devil chasing after me. Maybe he was after one of you two," he said, studying us, hoping to find evidence of guilt in our expressions.

Lee admitted to smoking one of Feenie's cigarettes, but quickly declared that James already knew that, since they shared that same cigarette. After a minute or two of debate, they concluded that many kids their ages had smoked, and none, to their knowledge, had ever been visited by the devil. Then they both warned me that I had better not tell anybody about their smoking.

Finally, James said "I don't think any of the shit we're talking about even matters in the grand scheme of things involving the devil. I don't know why he showed his face, but I know I ain't going back in that

126

damned house until that sumbitch is gone and gone for good!"

At that point, we weren't far from Granny's Greenhouse. I didn't know if she was there or not, but I knew she was one person who was not afraid of the devil, or at least she didn't display any fear of him in front of her grandchildren. In fact, almost everyday, she seemed to *want* to do battle with him, telling him to "get out of her life and go back to the depths from whence he came." She said that since she was one of "God's children," the devil couldn't touch her, no matter how hard he tried.

We found Granny and Eddie outside. Eddie was weeding petunias, while Granny was making some sort of blue fertilizer mixture she used to sell to customers who came to her greenhouse. About half of the customers that bought plants also bought her fertilizer mixture.

Running toward Eddie, I bellowed "James saw the devil!" My heart beat even faster as I said it.

Eddie immediately jumped to his feet.

Thankfully, Granny overheard me, my goal in shouting my proclamation. "What are you talking about?" she asked, studying me carefully, trying to find indications of a prank.

I rambled "James came running out of the bedroom and the devil was chasing him and I was real scared and we ran all the way here 'cuz you go to church all the time and you will be able to fight him."

Taken aback by both what she had just heard and the nature in which the news was delivered, she stood for a moment with an incredulous look on her face. She stared out into the distance for a moment, then turned back to me and asked "did *you* see the devil?"

I never lied to Granny. Sometimes I never told her the whole story, but I never outright lied to her. She said that God knew when I lied, so it was useless to lie to a child of God.

"No, I didn't see him, but I know he was there. I think James must've scared him off when he came back into the house to get me. I literally couldn't move for a long time!"

Granny went over to talk to James. I turned to Eddie and said hurriedly "Eddie, I was scared to death. I actually peed my pants. I think I did it in the living room. Feenie's going to beat the crap out of me."

Granny came back over to me and said "I'm going to call Annabelle Casto to come and take me up to the house. We'll see what this devil wants. He was probably looking for food and just got lost."

I was confused. I thought the devil didn't have to eat. "Why did she say that?" I thought. Though I wasn't really sure, I knew that she knew a lot more about how to fight the devil than I did, so I didn't ask her any questions.

Annabelle Casto was Granny's best friend. She was a large lady in every sense of the word. Physically, she stood about five feet and eight inches and weighed upwards of three hundred pounds, provided she hadn't eaten breakfast. Her stories were frequently so exaggerated that one couldn't tell where truth ended and fiction began. Her car was bigger than any other I had ever seen. The only small thing I remember associated with her was her tiny, one bedroom apartment, into which she moved following the death of her husband. Even then, when she talked of her previous home, a modest, two bedroom ranch, she recalled it more of a spacious mansion so big she needed a maid to help her clean it.

Though she often went out of her way to try to impress people, I still liked her. I gave her the benefit of the doubt on her

128

stories. She told them with such conviction I think she actually believed what she said.

I used to go to her apartment to take out the trash, help her clean her place, and wash her car. I hadn't been there for over a year, since her son came home from serving in the military in some place called Vietnam.

She called Granny daily and they talked on the phone for hours. Though they really seemed to enjoy each other's company, I hope Granny didn't believe everything Mrs. Casto told her.

They talked about everything from the greenhouse to their various ailments, real and perceived. And though they got on each other's nerves occasionally, fights always lasted less than a few hours, with one or the other calling to apologize.

They even talked about other people, something Granny insisted people shouldn't do. Eddie used to say "Granny likes to talk the talk, but doesn't always walk the walk." He thought Granny was a bit of a hypocrite when it came to gossipers. He said that Granny told him God didn't approve of gossipers, but "she and Old Lady Casto sure do a lot of it."

Mrs. Casto arrived at the greenhouse about a half hour later. She and Granny went down the aisle between the geraniums and the marigolds and talked for a little bit. I figured they were talking about how to beat up the devil and get him out of the house. After a few minutes, Mrs. Casto looked back over toward me and James. "Let's go find this devil and ask him why he's terrorizing you kids," she said.

Still frightened, I had no desire to go back. "Anything that scared James to that extent would not go down easy," I thought. But Granny and Mrs. Casto were a formidable team. Together, I reckoned, they would be able to at least get the devil out of the house. "If nothing else, Mrs. Casto could sit on him and keep him pinned down until the police arrive," I thought, though I didn't have any idea what the police would be able to do with him.

It only took a few minutes to drive back to the house. Mrs. Casto pulled into the driveway far enough to catch shade from the big oak tree. She pulled herself out of the driver's seat, then opened the back door for me. Eddie and James slid across the seat, getting out of the car on my side.

The door to the house was still wide open. Neither James nor I was worried about closing it when we ran out of there earlier.

Granny entered first, clutching her purse by the straps, so she could swing it if she needed to. Mrs. Casto was right behind her, holding a big, light blue umbrella in her right hand. I wondered to myself if she planned to stab the devil with it.

James, Eddie, Lee and I stayed outside, near Mrs. Casto's car, debating what we going to do if the devil chased Mrs. Casto and Granny back out of the house. "If he comes chasing Granny out of the house, do we jump into the car and lock the doors, or do we take off running?" I asked. We decided that running was the best option.

After a few harrowing minutes, Mrs. Casto came to the front door with a troubled look on her face. Gasping, she declared "boys, I have both good news and bad news. The bad news is the devil got your grandmother and has taken her to Hell, where she'll have to be his slave and do his bidding for eternity. The good news is he promised to leave you kids alone from now on. He even shook on it. Even the devil is required to honor a handshake."

Eddie immediately sprinted up the stairs. I didn't know why, but he later said that he was going to get Granny back from the devil. Just then, Granny came to the door, saying "stop it Annabelle, can't you see that they're scared enough?"

Mrs. Casto agreed. She walked back into the living room and plopped herself down on the sofa, pleased with herself that she was able to exploit, to such benefit, Granny's failure to quickly make it to the front door.

Granny called us into the house. We made our way back to the bedroom where the devil had appeared. A hole formed in the wall, right where James said he saw the devil. Burn patterns, appearing to have started from inside the wall, flowed outward, giving me all the proof I needed. "See, Granny? The devil was here," I said.

She told Eddie and me to go outside and play. "James and I are going to try and figure how to keep the devil out from now on," she said.

About ten minutes later, James came out, steaming mad. He called Granny names under his breath. When I asked him what was wrong, he angrily replied "the old battle axe is calling me a liar. She's accusing me of putting the hole in the wall and tryin' to burn the house down."

James hardly ever got angry with Granny. Sometimes he argued with her over her daughter, but I don't remember him fighting with her over anything else. He said "now the old senile bat's going to go tell The Old Man that I tried to burn down the house. If I wanted to torch the damned place, I wouldn't hide in the bedroom and do it. I'd just throw some gas on the floor, light a match, and walk the hell away."

Granny came back out of the house. "James Howard, come here, now!" On those infrequent occasions when Granny addressed us by both first and middle names, it was understood that she was to be listened to. "I don't know what you saw in that room

131

today. But I believe that *you* believe you saw the devil. And I believe you were scared. The door is completely off of its hinges. I know Mike peed his pants. So, I'm not trying to say you made it up, nor am I trying to accuse you of anything." She went on to explain why she was having such trouble believing James' story, saying "you see, sometimes grown-ups don't see the devil the way you described him. Myself, I believe the devil probably looks like a regular man."

After about ten more minutes of talking, James had calmed down a bit. But he remained firm that he had seen the devil. I believe he saw the devil. The terrified look in his eyes that day told me all I needed to know. I had never seen true fear in his eyes before or since. He knocked a door right off its hinges. I could only reason he did it to prevent the devil from grabbing him and dragging him to Hell.

The next couple of days were tense. Nobody wanted to sleep in that room. The four of us, Lee, Eddie, James and I each took turns staying awake, keeping an eye out for anything out of the ordinary. We reasoned that if one of us was awake and something came to get us, then we'd all wake up and beat the hell out of it, or at least run and get The Old Man so he could help us.

As time wore on, general fear turned to mild apprehension, which gradually faded. Before long, we all slept through the night without one of us standing guard. Less than a month after that incident, any or all of us slept there without worrying too much about the devil revisiting us.

The next few weeks were uneventful. We fell back into our routines, with each of us doing our assigned chores, and trying to stay out of Feenie's way. Life returned to normal, but not for too long.

Chapter 14: The Watch

Eddie and I were playing a rock baseball in the road in front of the house. As I tossed him little mounds of dirt, he hit them over into the field. Holding the semi-straight tree branch in hand, he imagined himself as Joe Morgan, a slugger for the Cincinnati Reds. I imagined myself Jim Palmer, a pitcher for the Baltimore Orioles.

He slapped one that went foul. I never gave much thought to it as it headed toward the house. After all, it was probably the fifth or sixth one hit in that direction.

A rock must have been contained inside, because the kitchen window shattered the very instant the clump made contact. It figures the only clump that didn't break apart when he hit it was the one that hit the window.

Fearing a severe ass whipping, we ran and hid on the east side of the house. We just made it around the corner before we heard that all-too-familiar scream. Within moments, it came. "Michael Steven and Eddie Ray, get your asses over here right now!"

Eddie peeked his head around the corner of the house and saw Feenie carefully looking about, trying to locate us. He quickly tucked his head back when he saw her scanning in our direction. He whispered "look, we might as well go in and get it over with."

I generally preferred to delay the inevitable, if for no other reason than to deny either of my parents the chance to immediately quench their thirsts for revenge. But Eddie quickly grew anxious when we did something that justified a butt whipping, insisting that since we knew we were going to get beaten, we should get it over with as quickly as possible. "Waitin' for the beating is far worse for me than the beating itself is," he explained. Since the day he nearly hyperventilated while awaiting punishment, I joined him in getting it over with quickly.

As we slowly made our way to the porch, I glanced over at Eddie. His eyes told me, as they frequently did, that he wanted to get his beating over with first. Come to think of it, "frequently" is not the operative word. He *always* wanted to get his over with first. Either he didn't much like watching his brothers getting whipped, or he didn't want to watch what he knew soon would be happening to him. I think it may have been a little of both, but more of the former. Even after he took a good beating, he kept his eyes closed while running around, wailing.

Feenie stood on the porch, her hair rolled up in big pink curlers and some kind of whitish-yellow skin mask on. She held one of The Old Man's leather work belts in her right hand, tapping her left hand with it. As soon as Eddie got within her reach, she grabbed him by the hair, jerked him close to her, ripped his pants down and whipped him furiously for about ten or twelve good licks. After she was done with him, she gave me an equally brutal one.

She sent us to the bedroom. James was already there, having fought with Lee yet again, that time over him not cleaning his mess after making a peanut butter and jelly sandwich. Lying on the bottom bunk, he read a comic book he said one of his friends let him borrow.

Eddie and I agreed we probably deserved to get our butts whipped for breaking the window. But we still called her every name we could think of, even chuckling at some of the names we made up. "Stinky butt dwarf," uttered Eddie. "Wicked Witch of Highland Park," I replied. James rattled off a tongue-twisting list of his preferred vulgarities, causing both me and Eddie to stop and take notice. Knowing we couldn't put together anything to challenge his tirade, we moved on to other topics. We talked about the old shack and the creek in Cravensdale, crawdad hunting, and, for some reason, Tink and Sis.

The Old Man made it home that night at about eight thirty. He must have had a pretty rough day at work. We fully expected him to storm into the bedroom. When Feenie told him what we did, he did just that. We fully expected to get a stern lecture. Again, he didn't disappoint.

What we didn't expect was being jerked out of the room and carried around like a couple of rag dolls. "I'm sick and tired of paying for shit like this," he screamed as he carried us into the living room. He had Eddie by the back of his jean shorts. He carried me with his right hand under my left armpit.

He threw us down onto the couch, causing Eddie and me to hit our heads together when we landed. He yelled "you little bastards are going to stop tearing shit up!" Removing his belt, he reached down, grabbed Eddie's arm, jerked him up and started wailing. Eddie ran around in circles, throwing his arm down to soften the blows, but The Old Man just kept lashing into him. He must have landed fifteen good shots on Eddie's already welted back side. Eddie ran to the bedroom screaming as soon as The Old Man let him go.

He furiously lashed into me about fifteen good licks. I don't know if it was because we had our asses beat only a few hours before or if it was because he was real mad, but that one hurt more than most I could remember. Either way, I screamed loud enough to show him he had definitely made his point, short-lived as it might prove to be.

Shortly after he finished, he stormed back into the bedroom. We cowered, whimpering like beaten dogs. As he stood over us, he screamed for a while and called us names. I don't remember much of what he was saying. My butt was on fire. I just wanted him to leave the bedroom. I didn't want to be around him or Feenie. I don't think Eddie did either.

As soon as he left, Eddie pulled his shorts down to look at the new welts forming on his butt and legs. He even had a few on his arms from where he was trying to protect his butt. Both of us sniveled for quite a while from the stinging pain. I showed him my welts. I had just as many as he did. I don't know why, but it seemed to help ease my pain when I saw he had the same welts as I did. He usually calmed down when he saw mine.

James said very little about the beatings that evening, preferring to read his comic his book over commiserating with us. The only thing he offered was "hey, I have faith that you two will find a way to get even."

Eddie was both hurt and mad, insisting it wasn't fair to get beaten so much for one stupid window. He said we had to do something. At the time, I didn't understand what he meant when he said "the punishment didn't fit the crime." Now that I'm older, I fully understand that concept.

The next day, Feenie took Jeff and Tim and went to town. James was working at the bakery. Lee was doing the dishes. Eddie and I were told to hoe the garden. Before we went out, we showed Lee our bruises and welts we received courtesy of Feenie and The Old Man the night before. We told Lee we thought it wasn't right to get beaten so much just for one window. Lee agreed, but didn't know what he could do to help.

Eddie had gone to the bathroom while I was talking to Lee. I was just about to make a peanut butter sandwich when I heard Eddie calling me from the hallway. "Mike, c'mere," he said in a hushed tone.

I went back to see what he wanted to show me. He had opened the door to The Old Man and Feenie's room. He pointed to a very nice silver watch sitting on the dresser. Even though I was standing eight feet or so from it, I could easily see the sharply defined black hands and Roman numerals against the display's white background. The time was just a little more than half past eight.

"Whose is it?" I asked.

"Looks like it belongs to The Old Man. And we ought to take it for him beatin' us so much last night," he declared.

I agreed, though I told him maybe we ought to give it a couple of days. But Eddie wanted to take it right then, saying we might not get the chance if we waited. If someone did something to Eddie he thought was unfair, he'd say so, and demand justice. If he felt the offense was really unfair, that justice had to be swift. Somehow, he'd get me to agree, and we would devise a scheme to make things fair again.

We knew we'd get into a lot of trouble for taking the watch, but we took it anyway, figuring that would even things out.

I put the watch on my right hand, admiring its detail and workmanship as we made our way to the garden. Eddie started to dig a hole, and we talked about what was going to happen when The Old Man found it gone. I told him "he's gonna really beat our asses for this one. We've never taken his stuff before. You sure you want to do this?"

Eddie stopped digging and said determinedly "don't care. It's just another ass beating. Hurts like hell at first, but we'll get over it. Besides, if it gets real bad, we'll just dig it up and give it back." I was pleased to hear he at least considered things might get that bad for us.

After we buried the watch, we began to hoe the garden. Though the size of the garden suggested that two people would have to steadily work for a day and a half to finish, Eddie and I could hoe it in one long day. We declared Thursday to be hoeing day. We knew it would be grueling, but we resolved to do it all in one day, so we could spend the rest of the week catching worms or tadpoles.

By the time we finished, it was already early evening. We had worked through the day, to the point that the watch we buried so much earlier wasn't much a part of our conversation. We talked about catching fireflies.

Feenie got back around six thirty or so. She inspected our work and didn't say anything, so I guess it met her standards. She wasn't the one we were worried about that night. We were worried The Old Man would go mad when he discovered his watch gone.

He made it home sometime after a quarter past seven. He took a shower. He had already been in the bedroom once and hadn't noticed the missing watch. After supper, he left, going over to help Old Man Teter work on his sixty-two Chevy truck. Eddie and I spent the evening catching about thirty fireflies.

We worried over the next few days, certain that at any moment he would notice the watch and raise "living hell." One day passed without him noticing it was gone. Then another one went by. After the third day, I had forgotten about it. Eddie never said much about it either, so I figure he forgot too.

Then one night about a month or so later, The Old Man came storming out of the bedroom, screaming "which one of you little bastards took my watch?"

In the month that passed since we took the watch until he finally discovered it gone, every one of us got our asses beat a number of times, and any of us had reason to take it and bury it or break it or just give it away.

He first turned to Lee. "Where's my watch, you little klepto?"

Lee, confused, said "I didn't even know you had a watch."

The Old Man turned to James. "If you took it, you better tell me now. Otherwise, it's going to get real ugly for you."

James shot back "I didn't take your goddamned watch. If I did, it'd be in pieces on the porch."

I thought The Old Man was going to backhand him as he did so many times before for his belligerence, but he just kept going from one brother to the next, trying to get a confession. Eddie and I both told him we never saw the watch.

Since he didn't find anyone feeling a pressing need to confess, he said "ok you little bastards. You know what to do. Line your asses up, youngest to oldest." His system was simple. He would lash into us with the leather belt one time for each year we had managed to survive on this earth. I was ten, so I got ten whacks. Eddie was nine, so he got nine whacks, and so on.

We lined up as instructed. Usually that was the time when the offender confessed. Sure, there were plenty of times he beat all of our asses and still got no confession. But slightly more often than not, the offender confessed, sparing the innocent an unwarranted beating.

Before he began the whippings, he shouted "one final chance! Anyone got anything to say? I'm going to count to ten, then I'm going to start whipping some ass."

As he began counting, I looked at Eddie, trying to get a read on his body language. Since he didn't make eye contact, I had a tough time trying to figure out whether he felt that was one of those times when a confession was warranted. I admit, though he was younger, on matters of punishment and fairness, I usually deferred to his reasoning. I stood silent and hoped he wouldn't crack.

The Old Man was counting in his usual cadence, shouting a number out, pausing two seconds, then shouting out the number that followed. "Three," he shouted, walking past me as he continued to inspect the formation for signs of someone ready to break. "Four!"

He made it all the way to eight before Eddie blurted out "we did it! We took it a long time ago and buried it, the day after you whipped us for breaking the kitchen window."

I didn't like it, but I understood why he confessed. There existed an unwritten code amongst the kids. If someone wasn't the offender, and was too beat up to take another beating, then the true offender had to fess up. Eddie later said he confessed for two reasons. One, James took a pretty good beating from The Old Man the previous night, and while he could handle yet another, he didn't deserve another one on our account. Two, Lee received a particularly brutal one from Feenie for breaking yet another plate while washing dishes earlier in the day, and needed some time to heal. "I figured we owed it to both of 'em, but especially to Lee," he told me.

The Old Man grabbed Eddie's arm and started wailing on him, shouting "where's it at, boy?"

Eddie, crying, shouted "it's in the garden!"

The Old Man gave me my beating, then told us to get our asses up to the garden and get his watch.

Even though it had only been a month or so since we buried it, we could not remember exactly where it was. We knew it was somewhere in the potato rows, but we couldn't remember if it was between rows three and four, four and five, or two and three. It had rained several times since we buried it, and the garden looked uniform. There were no fresh spots to indicate the ground had been dug up recently. I know – you'd figure we'd remember a simple thing like the location of a buried watch, especially one we knew could eventually cause us much trouble. But so much happened since we buried it. Between James' encounter with the devil and the bobcat incident, I guess we had completely forgotten about the watch.

Eddie and I spent the next three days and nights looking for that watch. We didn't look very hard during the day, but we made sure we were in the garden, digging, when The Old Man got home from work. We had a trouble light set up so we could dig at night. We dug from the time he got home until he fell asleep for each of the next two nights.

When he got home from work on the third day, he came up to the garden. By that time, we had dug up every inch of dirt between every row of potatoes. He said "you boys stay the hell away from my stuff from now on, you hear?" After Eddie and I both said "yes, sir," he told us to put the shovels in the shed and get our asses to bed.

Strangely, Eddie and I have rarely talked about that incident in the last few weeks on the telephone.

Not long after that, three days after school started, Feenie left for the final time. I think we all knew she would eventually leave for good. She had come and gone at least seven times in the previous year, each time leaving for a couple of weeks, then coming home for a little while. Jeff and James confronted The Old Man each time she came back, asking "why do you always take her back?"

The Old Man had a very hard time explaining why. Though I knew it made The Old Man sad every time she left, I was always a bit disappointed when I came home to see she was back. At least when she was gone, the beatings subsided.

Chapter 15: Foster Care

I have no idea why anyone would choose social work as her career choice, especially those who work at Child Services. Child welfare workers are seen as meddling when investigating charges of abuse or neglect. They are run down if they don't investigate aggressively enough, and something happens to a child they're supposed to protect. They deal with parents who hate them. They are hated at least as much by the very children they try to help.

Mrs. Kroy was professional in every sense of the word. She never allowed herself to get emotionally attached to any of the kids she worked with. She rarely talked just for talking's sake. Every thing she said was to make a point, and that point was made quickly and matter-of-factly.

Her silver hair belied her age. Her slender body and smooth face framed a woman thirty-five years old or so, but she looked forty-five with that hair. Not that it should have mattered. She presented as distinguished, educated, and sophisticated. I hate to admit it under these circumstances, but I might have had a small crush on her.

James had met her before. She was recommended to The Old Man to help him tone down James' behavior at school. She seemed to think the motive for his fighting was more complicated than it presented. She couldn't accept that James simply refused to allow anyone to bully his brothers. He especially hated older bullies tormenting his younger brothers. Fighting was simply his manner of communicating that hatred.

James never spoke badly of her. He called her "an old battle axe," but never expressed any desire to harm her, like he did Feenie.

Nearly six weeks had passed since we last saw Feenie. The Old Man managed to keep it all together for about three weeks, but eventually things inched out of control. Soon, there was little order in the house at any time when The Old Man was at work. Fighting one another daily, we broke much of what Feenie hadn't taken with her. Jeff and James went at it almost every day, putting a hole or two in nearly every sheetrock wall in the house.

Mrs. Kroy began coming to school each Monday and Thursday to check up on us. She usually wanted the same information each time she visited. She wanted to know when I last took a bath. She asked about what I had eaten since her previous visit. Finally, she seemed especially interested in how my brothers were adjusting to life without Feenie.

On Tuesday morning of the sixth week, she told me she was ordered to find "loving homes" for the six youngest of the children. She said since no families were willing to take in six brothers, we had to be split up. "I've already spoken to all of your brothers, except Lee and Jeff. I'm going to the junior high next to talk to them," she explained.

I was devastated. I spent the entire afternoon staring at the clock, waiting for the day to be done, so James, Eddie and I could talk. I expected it would be several days before she would split us up.

I was surprised to see her outside my classroom at three-thirty. I was horrified to learn she was taking me straight from school to a family I had never met.

"I ain't going nowhere but home!" I screamed.

Mrs. Kroy, ever composed, softly said "look, Mike, it's not permanent. It's only until your father can create some stability."

I didn't know what stability was, but I didn't need any of that. I just wanted to go home with my brothers.

"Eddie and James are on their way to homes right now," she said.

I won't ever forget that moment. Thoughts of not being able to see James and Eddie overwhelmed me. I instantly knew the family would never be whole again. I sat down on the floor and cried.

I was rarely one to cause a scene in school, save for fighting when the teasing became too much. But I have to say my crying, something nobody outside my family ever saw from me, drew a bit of attention that day. Thankfully, the curious kids were whisked along by teachers and the principal to their waiting busses.

After five minutes or so of my nonstop wailing, Mrs. Kroy offered her hand and said "come on, it won't be as bad as you think. You'll see."

Without Eddie and James, I really had no reason to go home. I imagined a lonely house, devoid of activity. I imagined The Old Man would be devastated when he got home. Granted, he always came home to utter chaos. And maybe he could have used some peace and quiet. But since Feenie left, he never seemed to get too angry, regardless of the condition in which he found the house. Besides, aren't seven unsupervised boys living in a tiny two bedroom house supposed to create chaos?

I agreed to go with her, but only on the condition she promised to let me visit Eddie and James. She said that shouldn't be a problem.

She stopped at the Five and Dime and bought a pair of pants and a shirt for me. She said "tomorrow, you'll be going to a new school. Wouldn't you like to show up in some nice clothes?"

I surveyed my clothes. My green and white striped shirt and brown corduroy pants were fine with me, even if they were dirty. Although I must admit I was a bit uncomfortable having to hold my left arm to my side so other kids wouldn't make fun of the large hole in the left underarm.

"What new school? I don't want to go to a new school. Besides, who's gonna help me understand schoolwork like Eddie does?"

She had no immediate answer. She paused for a while, then offered "if you have trouble understanding something, please tell your teacher. She can find resources to help you."

I sulked in the car all the way to my new home. Mrs. Kroy offered little sympathy. I asked her about a hundred times when I could see Eddie and James. She said "we need to get you situated in this home first and then we can talk about that."

I cannot say anything bad about my first family, Mr. and Mrs. Phares. Though they were far too young and busy to take in a child on a permanent basis, they agreed to keep me until Mrs. Kroy could find a more permanent home.

Mrs. Phares seemed saddened by my childhood experiences, and I did nothing to stop her from showering me with sympathy gifts. To their credit, neither she nor her husband yelled at me or hit me once in the three weeks I lived with them.

At my first permanent home, I learned a lot about being a personal servant. I grew to appreciate Lee's suffering.

Mrs. Vanderwier was very heavy. She never left her big, dark blue leather recliner, except to go to the bathroom. Neither she nor her sixteen year-old daughter seemed to want to do any work. That said, they put me to work doing just about everything that needed to be done, from washing the clothes and dishes, to scrubbing the soap scum out of the bath tub. Needless to say, I quickly grew to dislike them.

I hadn't been there five weeks when, after spilling hot coffee on "Momma Vanderwier" for the fourth time in that last week, I was removed and placed with the Gibsons, some thirty miles from my hometown.

I lived with the Gibsons for quite a while, far too often playing punching bag for their fourteen and fifteen year old sons.

When I went to visit James, I told him I was getting beat up a lot. He told me to do what I had to. I tried to stay far away from those two, since they were so much older and bigger than I. But they seemed to seek me out.

When Henry, the fourteen year old, awoke to a beautiful, big black snake slithering over him in the middle of the night, they felt they could no longer keep me. The two days I spent in the thick brush to capture that snake paid off handsomely.

My most memorable stint lasted all of two and a half days. I arrived at the Simmons' house on Saturday afternoon. Jim, their son, greeted me at the car. He said he was happy to have someone his age to play with. I was equally pleased I finally was placed with a family with a child my own age.

After we ate dinner that first evening, Jim and I threw a football, while he asked me lots of questions. I told him a bit about where I was from and about my family. I had no real answer for "what happened to your mom?"

The next day I was taken to church. The pastor delivered a hearty sermon, talking about "the need for a revival." After the service, he welcomed me and talked about the power of prayer. "Son, if you believe in God's infinite power, your prayers will be answered," he proclaimed.

I sorely missed my brothers. "Maybe God could put us back together," I thought. I prayed a lot all day Sunday and Sunday night.

When Monday came, Mr. Simmons woke me and Jim up early to start working his huge garden. We hoed from around six until about ten. My hands started to blister, and I was thirsty. I walked back to the house to get some gloves and some water.

Mr. Simmons was working on his truck. As I passed him, he asked "where the hell are you going?" His angry tone resembled nothing I had heard the previous two days. While Eddie likely would have sensed him capable of abrupt change from the moment he met him, I actually had to wait for the change to occur.

Continuing to make my way to the house, I said "I'm really thirsty and my hands have blisters. I'm gonna get some water and gloves."

Suddenly, I felt a horrible jolt of excruciating pain rush though my body. I fell to the ground and immediately curled up into the fetal position. My hands and feet tingled.

It took several seconds for me to realize what happened. Old Man Simmons had just kicked me square in the ass as hard as he could with a steel-toed boot.

I lay there writhing in pain for some five full minutes. I really felt like I was going to be paralyzed.

As I was regaining my wits, he stood over me. Taking off his leather work gloves, he hollered "you never turn your back on me, especially when I'm talkin' to you. YOU GOT THAT?"

I couldn't answer. I was literally dry heaving, having already vomited twice.

"Now, get some water and get back to hoein'. You hoe to sundown. Then you hoe tomorrow. These boots'll make sure of that."

Still feeling nauseous, I made my way into the house and got my water. After drinking three full glasses, I poured a little on my head to help me regain my senses. I thought about Eddie. I hoped he was doing better than I. Then I thought about James. *James would make that fucker pay!*

Looking through the kitchen window, I saw that bastard demonstrating to his boy just how and where he kicked me. They laughed as he demonstrated my having completely left the ground from the force of his kick.

I could accept that he was mean. Hell, most of the men I'd ever met were mean. But to laugh about it with his son was, well – please pardon my language – fucked up! Even Feenie didn't derive that much pleasure from beating my ass. I had to do something.

He left his son and went back to working on his truck. I gingerly made my way back to the garden. Jim stood there, leaning on his hoe. "Guess I should've warned you. Monday through Saturday he's pretty tough," he explained.

I looked at him, enraged. I literally bit a hole into my bottom lip. I said "well, you've been using that hoe as a fuckin' standing stick all morning, but your ass ain't in pain. Besides, I saw you laughing. What the hell is so funny about an old fat bastard beating up an eleven year old skinny kid? My old man would kick the shit out of him."

Jim looked astonished that I still had any fight left in me. He said "I'm going to tell him what you called him."

I responded "you won't make it before I split your head open with this hoe."

He angrily replied "don't talk about my dad like that."

148

I actually admired him a bit for defending such a pathetic-loser-hypocrite-piece-of-shit. But admiration and affection are two different things, and I was sorely lacking the latter.

I acted as though I was going to put some lime down. I grabbed two hands full. It burned like hell on my blistered hands, but I was not going to put it down. It had a purpose.

Jim turned to say something. Before he could utter a complete word, I threw the lime. It slammed into his eyes and nose. He spit what he could out of his mouth. He started screaming.

Roughly two hundred yards separated us from his prick of a father. I picked the hoe up. I thought for a moment about slamming the blade into the back of his whining, crybaby son, but I didn't. I rotated it and smacked him in his lower back, as hard as I could, with the wood end. He fell to his knees, crying for his dad. As the fat pile-of-shit ran toward me, I raised the wood and brought it down, with all my strength, onto his son's shoulder, causing him to scream in pain. His pathetic old man yelled for me to stop.

When the bastard got to within thirty yards, I put the hoe down and ran through the garden, about a hundred yards. With that much head start, he could never catch me. I picked up a three pound rock, and yelled at him to send his crybaby son to come get me. He dared not. I think he feared I'd finish him off.

So there we were, in a modern day standoff in the Simmons' garden. "What the fuck is your problem?" the pathetic, fat bastard screamed.

"Hey," I yelled back at him. "I just did to him what you did to me. I turned my back on you and you nearly killed me. He turned his back on me and he paid the price. He'll pay every time you think you need to mess with me. You hurt me, I'll hurt him more. If we keep goin', one of us is going to die. I'm ready. Is he?"

He stood there in disbelief. I think he really believed I was going to kill his son. I really didn't have it in me, but it sure felt good to put that bastard in his place.

He took his son to the house. I stayed at the far end of the garden, under the big maple tree. I sat so I could keep my eyes focused on the house. I didn't want him sneaking up on me. Neither he nor his son came back out of the house for the rest of the morning.

By early afternoon, Ms. Kroy was at the house to take me away. I tried to explain how he kicked me in the butt with steel-toed boots. She finally understood when I pulled down my pants and showed her my purple ass. She asked me what I had done to make him so angry. I told her I committed the unforgiveable sin of not being his biological son.

"You boys are having a tough time finding suitable families," she explained. "Please try and understand your father needs some time to get his life in order. I want to put the family back together, but I can't right now."

I thought for a moment about how to best appeal to her. "Look, Mrs. Kroy, I just want to be with my brothers. We didn't do anything to deserve this life. Why are you doing this? Why can't you take me to my dad's house?"

She paused for a moment, sighed, then said "your father is not capable of taking care of seven boys and holding down two jobs. He came to us and asked for help."

I didn't believe her. I couldn't. *How could he? We were his flesh and blood. He just had to try harder. Parents take care of their children, no matter what it takes.*

When we reached the stop light at Second Street, I jumped out of the car and took off running. It took her and her coworkers down at the child welfare office almost the entire afternoon to catch me. I ended up getting spotted behind the laundry mat.

Mrs. Kroy told me it was going to take some time for her to find me another home. In the meantime, I would be staying at my great aunt and my uncle's place.

Chapter 16: Aunt Marilee and Uncle Charlie

I never bothered to ask Aunt Marilee why her son, who was as old as my father, still lived with her. I just assumed she needed him around. Though not frail, her severe arthritis sometimes got so bad it left her toes curled, rendering her unable to walk.

They lived at the foot of Reese Hill Road. Every time we visited, Aunt Marilee gave us delicious snacks. She sometimes had cake. At other times, she had homemade cookies. Still others, she had pork rinds. She seemed to really like pork rinds. While they weren't as tasty as chocolate cake or homemade oatmeal cookies, they were still pretty good. I know none of my brothers ever turned down an offer of anything she offered.

Charlie often played a game where he'd squeeze our hands until we begged him to stop. We played that game many times with The Old Man, as well as with other friends and relatives. Eddie would play with just about everyone, but never with Charlie. I really couldn't tell any difference in how hard Charlie squeezed compared to how hard my dad squeezed. Eddie said it wasn't about the squeezing. It was about the reaction to seeing us in pain. He said The Old Man squeezed to show who was boss, but Charlie did it because he liked to see us in pain. He said Charlie was a mean son-of-a-bitch. He always stayed as far away as he could when we visited.

Aunt Marilee seemed gentle enough. She rarely gave any outward indication she was anything but a nice old lady. She came across as such.

As was routine, Eddie asked Aunt Marilee a lot of questions, most of which regarded her son. He asked about Charlie's speech impediment. He asked about Charlie's mood swings, and if Charlie had to take medicine. If he felt she wasn't completely forthcoming, he would continue on, probing ever deeper.

Once, he either hit a nerve, or clearly went beyond what she felt was appropriate. When he asked if Charlie ever finished grade school, she responded bluntly "you should learn to mind your own business."

I don't know if she just didn't have enough energy for all of Eddie's questions, or if she was embarrassed to answer that one, but that was the only time I heard anger in her voice. Following that, Eddie stopped asking questions, until the following visit.

But that didn't prevent him from observing her every move. He said she was tough to figure out. He said at times he believed her to be harmless, while other times he sensed she wasn't the nice old lady we had come to know. He told that to The Old Man, prompting a half-hour long lecture about him sticking his nose in where it didn't belong.

I learned to trust Eddie's instincts. I don't know how he figured people out, but he had a way of just knowing what people's intentions were by looking in their eyes, at their faces. Far more often than not, he was right about people. Everyone feared Ms. Blake, but Eddie said she wasn't mean, just in a lot of pain. She ended up being the one person we could count on for a peanut butter sandwich or a sloppy joe when we were starving. She went out of her way to help, even though she was as poor as we were.

I still think he was wrong about the Waybrights. I don't think Old Man Waybright was the one who Tony feared. I think it was his mom. I spent a little bit of time over at Tony's house, and never once witnessed his dad treating him badly, or even unfairly. And though I never saw his mom beat him, I did see her deny him everything from food to clothing, affording Tony such luxuries only after she ensured Tony's older brother got his fill.

On most days, Aunt Marilee's arthritis didn't prevent her from getting up and about. However, her hands never resembled anything one could consider *normal*. Her fingers were in terrible shape. They locked in various states of contortion, preventing her from performing even routine tasks others took for granted. As therapy, she put together jigsaw puzzles.

Eddie's gut instincts aside, I had no reason to fear anyone in the home. I'd been alone in the house many times, though never for more than an afternoon, and never felt uncomfortable. I was actually happy they decided to take me in. I hoped I wouldn't have to go to another foster home before The Old Man could bring us all back home. At least with them, I was with people I knew. Granted, they weren't my brothers, but they were extended family, so I felt comfortable.

I arrived on Monday night, and spent four uneventful days shooting basketball and catching tadpoles. The Old Man made a visit last Saturday. He didn't stay long, just enough to gauge my health, and to ask Marilee if she needed anything to help her. He left to see Eddie, up at the White's. He promised he'd be back this Saturday to visit. I wish he had spent just a little more time with me, but I knew Eddie would be happy to see him.

I spent the better part of this past week shooting baskets into a garbage can. The ditch across the railroad tracks all but dried up by Wednesday. I don't know what happened to the tadpoles, but I didn't see any dried up remnants. I figured their moms took them to another ditch somewhere so they could continue to develop. Perhaps once the water dried up, they became easy pickings for the birds, though I don't remember seeing a huge number of birds over in that direction.

I walked up to Gilman on this past Monday, and out to Highland Park on Wednesday. Highland Park was about a two hour walk, but I knew some kids over there, with whom I played for three hours before heading back to Aunt Marilee's. Thursday came and went, with me spending most of my day exploring and looking forward to seeing The Old Man this Saturday. I couldn't wait to ask how Eddie and James were doing.

Today started off as each of the past nine did. I woke up around seven, made my bed, and took the trash out to the aluminum can sitting against the wall on the north side of the house. After that, I shot baskets into the other can, using their house as a backboard. Aunt Marilee called me in for biscuits and gravy about an hour later. After breakfast, I shot baskets for another hour or so, then went back inside to get some water and to go upstairs to pee.

In a very short time, my whole life took a devastating turn for the worse. While I have never been a fan of hyperbole, simply saying that things progressed badly would be an enormous understatement.

As I was standing there relieving myself and thinking about what to do for the rest of the day, Charlie came into the bathroom and closed the door. I immediately felt uncomfortable, somehow sensing his intentions weren't virtuous.

I tried to get past him and out the door, but he grabbed me by my arm so hard I could not get away. He threw me on the floor and got on top of me, pinning my arms down with his knees.

I screamed for Aunt Marilee. Charlie tried to cover my mouth with his hand to muffle my screams, but I managed to turn my head and scream again. I kicked and bucked and tried as hard as I could to get him off me.

I managed to bite his hand hard one time as he again tried to muffle my screams. He backhanded me hard, literally knocking me dizzy for a second or two. When I got my wits about me, I told him "you're gonna regret that. When my dad gets here tomorrow, you know you're gonna pay!" Usually a threat such as that would give any offender, but especially Charlie, serious cause for concern. After all, The Old Man once beat him to a pulp when they got into it while putting siding on Aunt Marilee's house. I was alarmed that he seemed unfazed.

I was deeply relieved to see the door crack open. "Thank God," I thought, fully expecting Marilee to put her son in his place. As I struggled to get out from under Charlie's weight, I looked up at her to beg her to make her son get off of me.

I immediately began to see things as Eddie saw them. In less than half a second of eye contact, I could tell she knew what was going to happen. Not only that, I also knew she was going to do nothing to stop it. I saw more evil in her than even Eddie thought might have filled her. Her eyes told me that what was about to happen was the reason they decided to allow me to stay with them in the first place. I sensed, too, that I was not the first.

I don't think she wanted to hear the screams that were to soon echo through the house, brought on at the hands of her forty-five year old son. I again cried out for her help as she grabbed the door handle.

She looked in one final time. Though her soul was dark, it must have contained a tiny sliver of humanity, evidenced when she told him in a hushed voice "take it easy on him, he's still very young." She slowly closed the door, taking care to turn the handle gently so as not to scuff the locking mechanism. After the weight of her body hit the third step on her way back downstairs, I resigned myself to my fate.

Charlie told me it would go a lot easier if I didn't fight. He put some lard on his penis. He ripped my pants down and, though I struggled as if my life depended on it, managed to wrestle me over onto my stomach. I cried and begged and pleaded for him to stop.

Oh God, it hurt. I hadn't felt that much pain since Old Man Simmons kicked me. But it was a different kind of pain. I thought of Eddie and how he said Charlie was an evil son of a bitch.

It took almost five minutes for him to finish. When he was done, he offered me a lollipop. I didn't know what I was supposed to do. I wanted to run out, but I figured he'd grab me and do it all over again. I took the lollipop and, in tremendous pain, walked as best I could past him with my head down. I was both furious and ashamed of what I just allowed to happen. Though I was young, I knew what just happened would forever change me and how I saw the world around me.

I ran to my room, crying. Twenty minutes passed and my butt was hurting. Something felt wrong.

I cannot explain why I even spoke to Aunt Marilee. Perhaps because though she allowed it to happen, I sensed she had the ultimate power, and she alone could prevent it from happening again. I told her my butt felt hot. She told me to go to sleep and that I'd feel better when I woke up. She promised to not let Charlie touch me again. She gave me a glass of milk and a brownie. I cried myself to sleep.

After sleeping for about thirty minutes or so, I woke up in pain. I went and sat on the toilet for thirty minutes, unable to poop, but desperately feeling the need to. When it finally pushed through, I was frightened to see blood accompanying it. I screamed for Aunt Marilee to come. She looked in the toilet and immediately grew a look of restrained concern. I told her I still felt really bad and that it hurt a lot. She said it probably would hurt for a little while longer, but by tomorrow I would feel better. "If it still hurts this bad tomorrow," she said "I'll take you over to see Dr. Luke."

I never truly expected she would take me to the doctor. Any reasonable doctor would quickly determine what happened, and her precious Charlie would be whisked away for raping a child. Of course, that is all assuming the police possessed a modicum of expertise. Though I've personally never had interaction with the police, I have heard far too many people protest their incompetence. The Old Man often said "the idiots that pass for police in this town couldn't pass a one question test if that question asked what their names were." I've also heard people claim the police were in the criminals' pockets. I still don't understand exactly what that means, but people often said it with conviction.

"But tomorrow is Saturday. The Old Man is coming to visit," I thought. I knew any outrageous claim I made against his cousin and aunt would be met with great skepticism. "But if I told him I was really sick, he might take me to the doctor. The doctor would then make the claim for me. That way, I won't be held responsible for telling the family secrets."

I never mentioned The Old Man's impending visit to Aunt Marilee. It was my ace in the hole.

We had green beans and pork chops for dinner. For all her faults, that evil witch could cook. I really liked the way she cooked green beans. She slow cooked them with lard and bacon until they were tender. By the time they were done, the bacon flavor made its way into the green beans. They were, without question, the best tasting cooked vegetable I'd ever eaten.

At the kitchen table, everyone was quiet. I sat on one side of the table, staring at the wall behind the unpopulated chairs that sat directly across from me. Marilee was at the head, while Charlie sat at the foot. I sat closer to Marilee. Charlie looked ashamed. Marilee was quiet. Not a single word was uttered. We didn't even take a moment to acknowledge God, as we had for every meal until then.

Frankly, I wasn't all that hungry. But I didn't want to incite any anger that might have hidden in either of them, so I ate green beans, one at a time.

Suddenly, I had to run to the bathroom. I really felt the need to empty my bowels. The very moment I sat down, I felt my butt burning as poop and blood made its way out. I yelled toward the kitchen "Aunt Marilee! I'm bleeding again!" I was both scared and feeling a little faint. I asked her to call an ambulance.

She comforted me. She handed me a couple of pills and said "Mike, it's getting late. Take these aspirin. I promise you'll feel better by morning. Go on to your room and try to sleep."

I took the pills and then went to my room. Trying to be as quiet as possible, I pushed the dresser in front of the door, trying to lodge it between the wall and the door handle. At the very least, it would give me a pretty healthy head start out the window and into the woods if that son of a bitch tried to get at me again. I couldn't sleep. I thought "what am I going to do?"

I reflected on the day's events. I was angry and ashamed. Hurting both physically and emotionally, I cried for at least an hour. I thought of sneaking out of the window, but the night was already very dark. Unsure I would be able to make it the eight miles to town without getting attacked by a bobcat or a bear, I had to think of something else.

"I will just stay awake tonight," I thought. I had done it before. Sure, I didn't feel good the next day, but it was nothing a good night's sleep the following night couldn't cure. "Yeah, that's it. I'll stay awake and sneak out at first light, before they wake up."

Now that I had a plan, all I had to do was wait. I decided I would not leave the room, no matter what. If either of them came to the door, I would pretend I was

159

asleep. If they tried to get in, I would jump out the window and head off into the woods. If I had to go to pee, I would pee out the window. If I had to poop, then the pillow case would just have to be sacrificed.

I made conversation with myself, murmuring answers to my own questions.

As midnight approached, I started to feel a bit better. My butt still hurt a bit, but I had a little over four hours to go before I got out of there. "If I leave at first light, I can make it to Granny's Greenhouse by eight. I'll tell her – no, I'll *show* her what happened. She'll make sure Charlie won't get me," I thought.

I thought about Eddie and James and Lee. I wished James had been here earlier. He would have smacked Charlie up aside the head with a pipe wrench or a baseball bat. I imagined Charlie on the floor, curled in the fetal position, begging James to spare his life. The thought made me feel better.

About one-thirty, I started to grow very sleepy. "Please, not tonight," I thought. The day's events must have worn me down. My eyes grew heavy. I fought it as hard as I could. I couldn't to go to sleep, no matter what. I needed to be up at first light, so I could run away.

After ten more minutes, I could no longer fight it. I badly needed to sleep. "If I lay down," I thought, "I won't wake up in time to get away. If I'm sitting, I'll just drift off for a few minutes."

So I sat straight up and allowed myself to drift off for desperately needed nap.

Sometime later, I awoke to somebody moving about the room, shining a flashlight. I wondered how anyone could have made it into the room without waking me. "Aunt Marilee?" I asked.

I was relieved that it was she, and not her son, who responded. "Yes it's me. I just came to check in on you. How are you feeling?"

I told her I was feeling a bit better. She asked if I felt like I still needed to go to the doctor. Sensing she was probing, trying to find out if I was going to tell on her son, I told her I no longer needed to see the doctor. I couldn't see her face, but I hoped I eased her concern enough to leave me alone. I reflected on the way she looked at me as she closed the door to the bathroom earlier in the day.

But none of that mattered anyway. I was awake again, and I could easily make it until morning. Inside, I was jubilant. I just needed to wait for her to go back to sleep, wait for the first sign of daylight, then be on my way to Granny's.

I have witnessed a lot in my short time here on Earth, but what happened immediately following can only be described as *disturbing beyond imagination.* Aunt Marilee shined the flashlight onto my face. "Do it, now!" I heard her shout.

Those three words will likely be the last three I will ever hear another human utter. Before I could process why she would say that, I saw a big flash and heard a loud *boom.* I suddenly was blinded.

Oh, sweet Jesus! My great aunt just told her no-good-pile-of-shit-son-of-a-bitch-pedophile son to shoot me in the head. And he did it, without hesitation!

The bullet must not have hit me where they planned. I'm sure they both expected that I'd die immediately. But God, in His infinite mercy, has kept me alive for some three minutes, just long enough to allow me reflect on my short life, and to say my final goodbyes.

It is becoming harder and harder to take in anything other than rapid shallow breaths. I can't see anything. I must be bleeding badly, because I can now feel myself quickly growing faint. Eddie, if you can hear me, please make this right! James, I know if you were here, there would be two more dead people.

At least Charlie won't be able to hurt me anymore. Wait, what if he rapes me again after I'm dead? Will I feel it? Probably not. I don't feel the pain in my butt anymore. In fact, I don't feel physical pain at all.

I hear noises, but I can't make them out. I think Marilee and Charlie are talking. I think they are talking about what they are going to do with my body. I can't make out where they say they are going to put me. I hope it won't be too long before someone finds me.

My final thought returns me to the day Eddie and I met the Indian on the creek. Maybe the Indian man was my spirit guide into the next world. Maybe we were *meant* to find him. Yeah, that must be it.

Laboring as I draw my final, shallow breath, I go searching for him.

"Mr. Indian, are you out there?"

Made in the USA
Lexington, KY
18 July 2011

10368467R0